I0570787

Echoes of Tomorrow: Stories of Love, Regret, and Technology.

By Roxanne V.

© 2025 Roxanne V.

All rights reserved.

No part of this publication may be reproduced, stored in a retrieval system, or transmitted in any form or by any means—electronic, mechanical, photocopying, recording, or otherwise— without the prior written permission of the author, except in the case of brief quotations used in reviews or scholarly works.

ISBN: 978-1-0682719-1-5

This is a work of fiction. Names, characters, places, and incidents are either products of the author's imagination or used fictitiously. Any resemblance to actual persons, living or dead, events, or locales is purely coincidental.

Cover design by Roxanne V. with AI assistance

Published by Roxanne V.

Printed in the United Kingdom, London

*For my daughter, who taught me facets of love I never knew existed. *

Table of Contents

1. The Memory Architect..1

After her wife's death, Elena turns to technology to dull the pain — but when the love fades with it, she begins to wonder what mourning really means.

2. The Second Coming of Grace..8

A brilliant young woman resurrects her selfless mother through science, only to discover that love cannot be replicated — and regret cannot be undone.

3. Blue Harvest..24

Twenty years after creating the food-tech breakthrough that saved billions but left others starving, Dr. Iris Vey tries to dismantle the very system that made her famous.

4. The Loyal Ones..34

When love is monitored by implants and measured by neural syncs, Camille begins to suspect her perfect partner may be a perfect fiction.

5. The Father in the Mirror..55

A narcissistic absentee father uses AI to simulate the son he never raised — but when the real son appears, he must face a mirror that doesn't lie.

6. Thread-breaker..67

Born into a society of state-sanctioned soulmates, Kaela cuts the cord that binds her to a man she no longer trusts — and uncovers a secret about love, control, and autonomy.

7. Sleep Debt...86

In a world where the rich outsource sleep to the poor, two women become entangled through dreams neither of them is supposed to remember.

Story 1: The Memory Architect

Elena Myles sat in the chrome waiting room, her fingers lightly grazing the edge of a glass table that held nothing but a single white orchid. Everything smelled faintly of ozone and citrus. The walls pulsed gently with pale light, as if the room itself were breathing.

She had been here once before, months ago, not long after Rhea died. But she had walked out. Not today.

A woman in grey stepped into the room and smiled with engineered softness. "Ms. Myles. He's ready for you."

Elena rose without a word. Her boots made no sound on the frictionless floor.

The Architect's office looked more like a chapel than a clinic. A wide circular space with high, white vaults. At its centre, a single reclining chair — like a dentist's throne reimagined by a minimalist cult — faced a pane of living glass. Behind it stood Lucien Voigt, tall, silver-eyed, ageless. He smiled the way a blade might glint.

"Elena," he said, as if they were old friends. "You came back." She didn't smile.

"I'm ready now."

Lucien nodded, walking slowly around the chair.

"You understand what this entails? We don't delete memories. We rewire the pain — dull the emotional charge. The image stays, but the weight doesn't."

"I know," she said. Her voice felt detached, like she was listening to someone else speak. Lucien gestured to the chair.

"Then let's begin."

The first session was diagnostic. Lucien accessed her neural map through a cranial halo — a wreath of pale metal that hovered above her temples. He murmured quietly to his assistant, and images flickered briefly in the air: a watercolour of her mind.
He spoke as he worked.
"You and Rhea met at university?" "Yes."
"Fell in love quickly." "Yes."
"There were fights." "Yes."

One of them rose unbidden — the puppy. Rhea had wanted one for months: a ridiculous ball of fluff to brighten their quiet apartment. Elena had said no before Rhea could finish the sentence. Too loud. Too messy. Too much work. But Rhea's disappointment wasn't really about the dog. "It's not just a pet," she had said, eyes glossy. "It's something we could love together. Something that loves us back." Elena remembered brushing her off, going back to her emails, certain she was being reasonable. Even now, the silence that followed that night pulsed beneath the surface of her skin. It wasn't about the puppy. It was about how little room she'd made for softness.

He looked at her. "But love."
Elena closed her eyes. "Yes."
And there she was. Rhea.
Tall and willow-limbed, with burnished brown skin and tight curls she never bothered to tame. Her eyes were dark and curious, full of storm

2

and sweetness. There was something elemental about her — like gravity — as though even silence leaned in her direction. She wore oversized shirts, always half-buttoned, and smelled of bergamot and old paper.

Elena had been her opposite — precise, ivory-pale, angular, with sharp grey eyes and a habit of folding her sleeves exactly twice. She wore structured coats and clean silhouettes, her platinum-blonde hair always pinned or tied. Reserved. Disciplined. But behind the cool exterior was a hunger — for connection, for meaning — that only Rhea seemed to touch.

Where Rhea was jazz, Elena was architecture. But they met in the philosophy library, fingers brushing the same volume of Simone de Beauvoir, and something clicked — a current neither could explain. They had argued about ethics and poetry before their first kiss. Rhea had leaned in mid- sentence, mid-rant, and Elena hadn't stopped her. Rhea had called Elena her "iron orchid" — beautiful, cold, and secretly wild. Elena had called Rhea her "chaos compass" — always spinning, but somehow always leading her home.

The images sharpened:

Rhea's laughter in the rain. The red of her scarf. The salt of her neck. Her voice in the early hours of the morning: low, warm, laced with dreams. The way she used to dance barefoot in the kitchen when the world felt too heavy.

And then: the arguments. The slammed doors. Rhea sobbing in the hallway. The last voicemail—

Elena. I'm sorry. I can't keep doing this if you won't talk to me. I love you. Please—

Lucien paused.

"This will be one of the anchors. Do you wish to keep it?" Elena hesitated. Her lip trembled.

"No."

He tapped something into a screen. The memory dimmed, lost its edge. When she tried to recall it, it fluttered like a photograph left too long in the sun.

In the days that followed, Elena felt lighter.

The grief — sharp, debilitating — softened. She could walk past Rhea's favourite café without collapsing. She slept. Ate. Laughed at a movie. But the laughter felt like it belonged to someone else.

Then came the gaps.

One morning, she stared at a sweater on the bed and couldn't remember if it had been Rhea's or hers.

A friend asked how they'd met. She fumbled. "Library," she said. "I think."

She played their wedding video again. Rhea in a simple silk dress, sunlight caught in her hair. Her laugh — once a live wire — now sounded like a melody remembered, not felt.

She touched the screen.

"I remember loving you," she whispered. "I just don't remember how."

She returned to Lucien's office.

"Something's wrong," she said. Her voice shook. "It's like she's fading." Lucien folded his hands.

"You asked us to remove the charge. We did. What you're feeling is... absence." "But I don't feel her anymore."

"Pain is the anchor of love, Elena. Without it, the tether frays." "Can you reverse it?"

He looked regretful.

"No. Once we sever the emotional synapse, the brain reassigns the space. What you lost can't be regrown."

"You should've warned me."

"We did. Most people only hear what they want to hear."

Elena stood in silence. Her chest felt hollow — not aching, just empty.

"Do others regret it?"

Lucien's voice was quiet.

"Only the ones who loved deeply."

Mara came into her life gently, like dusk.

Mara was moonlight to Rhea's wildfire. Petite, freckled, with soft, round features and wide hazel eyes that blinked too often when nervous. She was a botanist. Quiet. Attentive. Thoughtful.

She made tea without asking. She listened more than she spoke. She offered no promises — only presence.

One night, after too much wine and shared silence, she asked, "Do you still love her?"

Elena thought a long time.

"I don't know. I remember that I did."

"That's something," Mara said, taking her hand. Elena looked at her fingers. Pale, slender, bloodless.

"I wish I missed her more," she whispered. "I want to miss her."

A month later, Elena found a memory stick tucked into a box of winter scarves. Rhea's handwriting on the label: do not open unless you miss me.

She watched the recording in darkness.

Rhea sat cross-legged in their old apartment, face flushed, eyes soft.

"Hey, Lena. If you're watching this, I'm probably gone. And knowing you, you'll have tried to bury it — to keep going. To survive."

A pause.

"But please, don't trade pain for emptiness. Love me loud. Love me honestly. Even the hard parts. That's the only way I'll stay real."

Elena stared at the image. Her throat burned. But no tears came.

She began writing.

Letters to Rhea. Journals. Fragments.

I remember your hands. I think. I remember being safe.

I'm not sure if I'm mourning you or the person I was when I loved you.

Does memory matter if the feeling is gone?

She started recording her dreams. In some, Rhea appeared — whole and radiant. In others, she was just a blur, a shadow laughing at the edges.

One day, Elena stopped speaking. Not out of sadness, but out of futility.

Friends called. She didn't answer.

Mara came by. Knocked. Left flowers. Then stopped.

A week later, Lucien Voigt received a sealed envelope. No return address.

Inside: a wedding photo. Two women laughing under a canopy of red silk. And a note.

Can you remove what's left?

On the back:

Elena Myles

Lucien sighed.

He turned the photo over in his hands. Then, slowly fed it into the scanner. The orchid in the waiting room had begun to bloom again.

He stood there a long while.

Outside, a woman in a brown coat walked past the glass wall and paused — face shadowed, posture familiar, a ginger Irish Setter puppy tucked under one arm.

Lucien blinked. But when he looked again, she was gone.

Just the orchid remained, its white petals catching the light like memory itself: beautiful, weightless, and almost real.

~ * ~

Story 2: The Second Coming of Grace

Part I: The Weight of Love

The day started like most others: with Grace on her knees, wiping synthetic marble tiles under flickering kitchen lights, and Sophie on the sofa, legs folded, eyes locked onto a holo- screen suspended in mid-air. It was 06:42. The cleaning drone had jammed again, and Grace didn't have time to fix it before her first shift. So, she scrubbed by hand, shoulders aching, hair tied in a lopsided bun that had seen better weeks. Her breath came out in foggy puffs—not from the cold, but from fatigue that no amount of hot coffee or over-the-counter stimulants could fight off.

Sophie barely noticed. Her fingers danced across the air, interacting with her augmented stream. Her face glowed blue from the screen, lips mouthing silent reactions to messages from friends whose names read like usernames: @Ivory.rose, @Miraklux, @TrueWest. One of them had just posted photos from a luxury VR gala in Kensington. Sophie zoomed in on a pair of custom silver ankle boots, tagged at £2,490.

"I need these," she muttered. "Everyone's got the new era-fades already." Grace looked up, still on her knees. "You need breakfast first." Sophie rolled her eyes. "There's no food anyway. The fridge is empty." "There are oat packets. And the machine's working again." "That's not food, that's punishment."

Sophie had always been like this — stunning to look at, sharp-minded, socially magnetic — but cold. Not cruel, exactly, just self-contained in a way that felt impermeable. From the moment she'd turned eleven, she'd begun treating love like a transaction. She expected, demanded, absorbed. Grace was the provider, the fixer, the ATM. Birthdays were lists.

School projects were emergencies for Grace to solve. Praise was accepted with indifference; criticism was met with doors slammed and silence.

Even when Grace had ended up in hospital twice the winter before — lungs tight, fever spiking, her body begging her to stop — Sophie hadn't visited. She hadn't even called until day two. Her voice had been drowsy on the other end of the line: "Sorry, Mum, I had this thing with Mary. We were up late." As if her mother's chest infection was a minor inconvenience, like a faulty charger. Grace hadn't cried — not where anyone could see. She'd blamed the antibiotics. Blamed the beeping of the machines. Blamed the bland food.

And when she finally let herself buy a small jar of imported honey, the kind she'd remembered from childhood sick days in her home country, Sophie had scoffed.

"Seriously? You spent that much on honey? That could've gone toward those PJ bottoms with the MarsBoy print. You know I wanted those!"

Grace had smiled. Weakly. Said nothing.

She'd wanted to say, *It's for my throat. I cough blood at night now.*

She'd wanted to say, *I needed something that reminded me life can be sweet.*

But what came out was, Maybe next month, if there's enough left.

What tormented Grace most wasn't the selfishness — it was the fear that Sophie had learned it from her. That maybe she'd failed to teach her daughter gratitude, empathy, or love in any language Sophie could understand. She had raised her alone, yes, but with tenderness: soft praise whispered in the dark, stories from a country Sophie never asked about, support for every dream, club, tutor, or tantrum. She spoke often of how proud she was, how beautiful Sophie was becoming, how the world would open its arms.

All she ever wanted in return was a hug. A spontaneous "I love you." A moment where Sophie would sit beside her and just... see her.
But the affection never came. Not even a hand squeeze. Not a glance of concern. Not once had Sophie stopped and said, Mum, are you okay? And so, Grace lay awake most nights, sore and coughing, curled around the ache of her own doubt, whispering into the dark:

"What did I do wrong?"

Grace stood slowly, wincing at the pull in her lower back. She walked over, wiped her hands on a towel, and smoothed a loose strand of Sophie's glossy hair—dark, sharp-edged, like her father's. Sophie flinched away. "Don't. You've got bleach on your hands."
Grace didn't take offense. She rarely did. "I'll try to pick up something from the discount box on my way back. After my second shift."
"You mean third," Sophie said flatly.

Grace smiled tiredly. "You're keeping count. That means you care."

"I just want to know when we'll have normal things. Like—like real food. A hover pod. An actual holiday."

"We live in one of the best zones in London. You've got access to tech most girls your age only dream of."

Sophie said nothing. Her eyes darted back to the screen, where her friends were already planning the next digital hangout—some new sensory lounge that cost more for an hour than Grace earned in half a week.

"Maybe if you just asked Dad again—" "No," Grace said. Sharp. Final. They didn't talk about him. Not because he was a monster or dead. But because he was worse: indifferent.

"I'm off," Grace added, softening. "Don't forget to log into school. And… if you could take the bins out, that'd help." Sophie waved vaguely, already half-immersed in the next stream. "Sure. Whatever." Grace watched her a moment longer, then slipped out the door.

Sophie didn't think she was a bad daughter — just a normal one. She was sixteen. She had stuff going on. Pressure. Exams. A social life to maintain. Friends who wouldn't stop uploading filtered versions of their perfect days — makeup drops, dance loops, parties in tech suites with ice-chilled drinks and synthwave playlists. It was exhausting keeping up. Everyone knew teenage years were supposed to be hard.

"I'm allowed to be selfish right now," she often told herself. "I'm figuring things out."

Besides, her mum didn't get it. She acted like oatmeal and clean floors were the answer to everything. She didn't understand how brutal it felt to show up at school in last-year trainers, or not have the newest AR filters, or miss out on Mary's rooftop birthday because you couldn't afford a token invite. Grace talked about hard work like it was sacred. But what did that ever get her? If Sophie ever thought about how her mum looked when she coughed into her elbow, or how she rubbed her wrists at night when she thought no one was watching — she brushed it aside. "She's a grown-up. That's what they do. They cope."

And so, she never asked how Grace was feeling. Never said thank you. Never offered to help, unless it came with a guilt-tripped eye roll or some transactional ask.

Because deep down, Sophie believed that being sixteen made her the center of the world. And her mother — constant, unshakable, quietly collapsing in the background — was just part of the scenery.

The news came by 17:03. A soft chime on Sophie's wrist interface. A hospital AI with a synthetic voice. Polite. Efficient. Inhuman.
"Ms. Grace Morgan, aged 42, has been involved in a collision. Life preservation efforts unsuccessful. Please confirm next of kin."
Sophie didn't understand it at first. She blinked, checked the message again, looked around the empty flat. A bowl of congealed oats still sat on the counter. The cheap lamp in the corner flickered like it always did. She re-read the word: unsuccessful.

She called her mum's number. No answer. Tried again. Nothing. She walked to the kitchen and vomited in the sink.

Part II: The Silence That Follows

The funeral was sparsely attended. Some of Grace's old friends and coworkers came, a weary-eyed man from the laundry unit who spoke in gentle murmurs and brought a wilted bouquet. A social worker hovered by the door, checking her holo-pad every few minutes, eyes glazed with sympathy fatigue. Sophie sat alone in the front row, face blank, dressed in borrowed black. No tears. No speech. Just a numbing weight that felt like static behind her eyes.

Afterwards, the flat was stripped within days. Government repossession. Too valuable a location to remain in the hands of someone who couldn't pay. The "Safe Haven Housing Act" allocated Sophie to a low-zone unit in Barking—a cubicle inside a shared accommodation tower where the walls were smart glass and the neighbours were ghosts.

The silence there was deafening. She would lie on her back at night, hearing only the faint buzz of circuitry in the walls and the distant screech of transit pods gliding down the express tracks. No one messaged. No one called. @Ivory.rose posted a tribute once—"So sad. RIP Grace "— then went back to streaming makeup tutorials and dating samlets.

Her inbox filled with unread job offers for entry-level positions: cleaning drone maintenance, VR warehouse cataloguing, content tagging for the algorithm. She picked the one that offered meal credits. Her first paycheck was half-docked for "introductory training." The next was cut due to low performance metrics.

She ate protein paste for dinner. Walked five kilometres when her metro credits ran out. Sold her old social avatar and all its curated skins just to afford a second-hand winter jacket. Still, she didn't cry.

But she did start thinking. A lot.

About how her mother used to come home with bloodshot eyes and still ask if she'd eaten. How she'd once stitched Sophie's torn hoodie in the middle of the night so she wouldn't be embarrassed at school. How she never took holidays, never bought anything for herself.

And how Sophie—stupid, distracted, selfish—had barely noticed.

She found herself replaying old memory captures from the flat's internal monitors. Her mother humming while cooking. Laughing at a broken kettle. Coughing in the dark, muffling the sound so Sophie wouldn't wake up.

Eventually, grief turned inward. Hardened into something dense and unbearable.

One evening, after a long shift spent sorting digital trash, she stood in front of a street mirror, staring at her reflection. Skin pale, hair limp, eyes unfamiliar.

"I'm not her," she whispered. "But maybe I can be better."

She enrolled in a city college using hardship grants. Her attendance was perfect. Grades shot upward. Nights blurred into early mornings over biology diagrams and neural sequencing

interfaces. By nineteen, she'd published a thesis on quantum memory anchoring. By twenty- three, she was leading research teams in synthetic consciousness preservation.

Her colleagues called her brilliant. Driven. Unshakable. They didn't know she was building a ghost.

Part III: A Mind Rebuilt

By the time Sophie turned twenty-six, she had become one of the youngest researchers in the Neural Synthesis Division of NeuroDyne Biologics — a company that flirted with the boundaries of the law like a cat plays with a mouse.

Officially, NeuroDyne specialized in long-term memory retrieval and neurological preservation. Unofficially, its black labs dabbled in forbidden domains: identity transfer, self-aware cloning, echo consciousness. Governments had banned full-mind replication following the 2041 incident in Osaka, but the tech had evolved faster than the ethics.

Sophie didn't care.

She'd read every scrap of data her mother had ever left behind. Harvested EM signatures from the old flat's smart walls, extracted trace personality patterns from obsolete medical scans, voice logs, the GPS heatmaps of her final years. She built a psychographic framework of Grace from scraps — not just what her mother did, but how she reacted, how she moved through the world.

And then she grew the body.

They called it a neoform — a biologically engineered construct indistinguishable from a human. Sophie used her own DNA as a base, filled the genome with every trace of Grace's chromosomal data she could legally access, and enhanced it with anti-degeneration markers. It looked exactly like her mother did at thirty-seven, the year before the tiredness became terminal.

She couldn't do it inside NeuroDyne, of course. That would be traced. So, she partnered with a freelance neuroarchitect in Prague, one who owed her more than a few favours. A private lab, unregulated. Quiet.

For eighteen months, Sophie worked on Grace in secret.

Every night, after meetings and lectures, after the lights dimmed and the city outside hummed with electric life, she would slip into the lab and sit beside the stasis pod.

Sometimes she would talk to the body curled inside, fingers twitching faintly beneath the nutrient gel. Sometimes she just watched. Waited.

Then, one morning, she woke to an alert on her neuroband.

"Neurological integration sequence: complete. Subject consciousness online."

Sophie barely remembered how she got there. Just the white corridors, the rush of her pulse, and the sound of her own footsteps echoing back at her like questions she wasn't ready to answer.

She opened the pod.

Grace blinked. Slowly. Her eyes — that warm grey Sophie had forgotten the exact shade of — adjusted to the light.

"Sophie?" she said, voice raspy but recognizably hers. Sophie choked on a breath.

"Mum."

There was a long pause. Then: "You've grown."

Sophie reached out, hand trembling, and touched her mother's arm. It was warm. Soft. Real. And for the first time in over a decade, Sophie cried.

They spent weeks inside the Prague hideout, the world narrowed to just two people — the living and the once-dead. Grace's mind, at first, was patchy. She remembered fragments: Sophie's childhood, old recipes, the smell of lavender detergent, the name of a cat they never owned. Sophie didn't care. She filled in the gaps, eagerly recounting their life together, everything she'd never said. How much she loved her. How sorry she was. What she'd built her life to become.

Grace listened, smiling, gentle. "You've done so well," she said once, stroking Sophie's cheek. "I'm proud of you."

It should have been enough. But it wasn't.

There were little things, small at first. Grace refused to cook. Said she hated the smell of kitchens. She didn't laugh the way Sophie remembered — not from the belly, but sharp, clipped, almost performative. She drank wine now, in the evenings, alone. Stared out the window like the city was calling her somewhere.

"You never drank," Sophie said once.

Grace shrugged. "I didn't have time, back then. I do now."

Then came the night Sophie found her mother dancing. Not the gentle sway she'd once done while folding laundry. This was something else — something fluid, sensual. She moved like a woman tasting freedom for the first time. A strange man watched from the corner, sipping gin, amused.

Grace looked up, unashamed.

"You never told me being alive could feel this good." Sophie said nothing.

Something had come back. But it wasn't the same. Not quite.

Part IV: Resurrection

By mid-autumn, Grace was living in Sophie's Kensington apartment — a sleek, minimalist space filled with recycled light and the faint smell of eucalyptus from the air filtration system. Sophie had prepared everything. The guest room was painted soft blue, filled with old photos, scent-triggered memory lamps, and a hand-programmed AI assistant that spoke with the same cadence as Grace's former home hub.

At first, it felt like a dream realized. They shared meals — or at least tried to. Grace often picked at her food, eyes scanning the skyline from the window. Sophie brought her books, vintage films, soft slippers. She wanted her mother to feel safe. To feel home.

But Grace didn't seem to want safety.

One afternoon, Sophie came home early from the lab to find Grace gone. No message. No ping. Just a half-drunk glass of citrus vodka on the table and her bedroom door left ajar.

Sophie activated the flat's search grid — a soft AI sweep of Grace's tracker node — and found her six blocks away, in an open-air bar on a high-rise roof. The woman who was once Grace was leaning over a railing, laughing, her hair tumbling in loose curls, a glass in her hand and a man's hand resting easily at her waist.

Sophie watched from a distance.

Grace caught her eye eventually and raised her glass in a casual toast. Then turned back to the man.

When Sophie confronted her later, she didn't yell. She couldn't. The disappointment tasted like ash in her throat.

"I thought you'd want to spend time together," she said. Grace peeled off her coat.

"I do. Sometimes."

"Do you remember why I brought you back?" Grace gave her a long, quiet look.

"I think," she said slowly, "you brought back an idea of me. Not me."

Sophie's jaw tensed. "You were kind. You worked until your fingers bled. You gave me everything."

Grace tilted her head, as though examining a child's logic. "Yes. That version of me did. But I'm not her. I'm... something new. Something free."

"You're my mother." "I'm your creation."

Silence stretched between them, taut and painful. Then Grace smiled. Soft. Inevitable.

"Maybe I don't want to be that anymore."

The days grew colder. Grace started spending nights away — first with the man from the bar, then another woman, then alone. She spoke of travel, music, sensation. She tried aerial yoga, fusion cuisine, skydiving simulations. Her wardrobe changed. Her voice even shifted, slowly — more casual, more irreverent.

Sophie watched the transformation with something like grief. It was the second death, this time slower.

She thought about shutting the system down. There were failsafes in place. The clone's consciousness was tied to a hybrid cloud-rooted network. It could be suspended, reset.

But she couldn't do it.

Because sometimes, late at night, Grace would return. Sit beside her. Hold her hand in silence. And for a moment, Sophie could pretend.

Until one day, Grace stood in the doorway, suitcase in hand. "I'm leaving."

Sophie didn't look up from her screen. "For how long?" "Indefinitely."

"Why?"

Grace smiled faintly. "Because you want me to be someone I'm not. Because I want more than what you remember. I'm not a memory, Sophie. I'm alive."

Sophie's voice cracked. "I made you because I loved you. I wanted to say sorry. I wanted to make it right."

"I know. But love... doesn't bind. It frees." Grace walked to the door. Before she left, she turned back once. Her voice was soft.

"Thank you for giving me a second chance. I hope you give yourself one, too." And then she was gone.

Part V: Alone, Again

The apartment was too quiet now.

Not the peaceful kind of quiet — but the vacuum left behind when a door closes and doesn't open again. The smart speakers no longer responded to Grace's voice profile. Her mug sat untouched on the counter, a faint lipstick mark still on the rim. The scent of her eucalyptus shampoo lingered for days, until Sophie finally turned off the vent system and opened every window. Cold air filled the space. She didn't mind.

She kept busy. Worked long hours, ran simulations, reviewed student papers, lectured on neuroethical paradoxes to rooms full of ambitious minds too young to see the trap in their own ambition. At night, she'd sit by the window, eyes dry, watching mothers on the street below —

laughing, scolding, tugging little hands across pedestrian bridges lit by the soft blue hue of eco-lamps.

They all looked like ghosts now.

She replayed the memory captures. Grace at twenty-five, laughing as she tried to do Sophie's pigtails and failing. Grace at thirty-eight, massaging her aching wrists in silence. Grace at forty-two, leaving for work in the dark.

Not the clone. Not the free spirit who walked away with her suitcase and her expensive new coat.

The real Grace. The one who sacrificed everything.

And the one Sophie never said thank you to — not really.

One night, weeks after Grace left, Sophie visited her old flat in Barking. It was condemned now. The hallway lights flickered. Her old room was gone — rebuilt into two micro-studios. But in the alley behind the building, someone had painted a mural across the brick: a woman pushing a shopping cart, head held high, face tired but noble.

She didn't know who painted it. Maybe no one did. She just stood there and whispered, "I'm sorry."

The wind picked up. Dust spiralled past her shoes. A piece of paper fluttered by — a local advert, crumpled and half-torn, promising a "rebirth package" from a competing biotech firm.

Sophie didn't pick it up.

She still worked. Still walked the halls of NeuroDyne like she owned them. But the obsession was gone now. The fever.

She didn't try to rebuild Grace again. She could have. She had the files. The sequences. Even the old stasis pod, still cold in storage.

But the truth sat in her now, fully digested.

Looking back, she realized she hadn't been a complicated teenager —
just a selfish one. The kind who confused drama with depth. Who
thought stress was a shield and being sixteen was an excuse. "I wasn't
going through a phase," she admitted to herself. "I was just... unkind."

And now, the apology she'd once found too awkward to say was the only
thing left echoing inside her.

Some things can't be brought back. Not really.

Love can drive you to rebuild the past, but it can't rewrite it. And regret
— the deepest kind — doesn't want resurrection. It wants forgiveness.

One morning, Sophie sat on a public bench outside the Southbank
Library. She watched a mother and daughter walk past, laughing at
something on a shared device. The daughter was maybe twelve. The
mother looked tired.
Still, she smiled.
Sophie smiled back.
Then she sat quietly, hands folded in her lap, and let the morning sun
warm her face. She didn't feel better.
But she felt awake.
And that, finally, was enough.

~ * ~

Story 3: Blue Harvest

This story will explore greed, legacy, and moral accountability, set in a richly imagined future where solving world hunger came at a corporate price — and now, years later, the inventor wants to undo the very thing that made her famous.

... *"We thought we'd saved the world. We just never asked who could afford salvation."*

Part I: The Invention

The night the world crowned her a saviour, Dr. Iris Vey stood beneath a cascade of artificial starlight, wearing a dress spun from lab-grown silk and guilt she hadn't yet learned to name.

Applause rippled through the glass rotunda as the announcement echoed above:

"Winner of the Nova Humanitarian Award, for outstanding contribution to the future of human survival — Dr. Iris Vey, creator of BlueYield."

She smiled, posed for photos, held the transparent trophy aloft. Cameras swirled. Wine flowed. The world had been burning, starving, cracking — and she had given it something green. Crops that grew on concrete. Nutrition engineered at the cellular level. Plants that needed no soil, no sun, no time. Just a patch of space and synthetic stimulation. And they worked. Just not for everyone.

Twenty years later.

Iris sat alone in a penthouse tower that filtered the sky to a pleasant shade of turquoise. The view was uninterrupted — no neighbours, no ads, just horizon — but she rarely looked out anymore. Below, London's "Growth Zones" shimmered in enforced green: tiered towers of engineered produce stacked like neon-lit beehives.

Somewhere on the fringes, in the "dry sectors," children still died clutching dust, dreaming of the taste of real apples.

BlueYield crops weren't grown there. Couldn't be. Not without licenses. Not without access to the nutrient codes — all property of AgriThena Global now.

She sipped her tea, lukewarm and floral, and watched the headlines scroll across her holo- wall:

Dakar: Food Riots Leave 9 Dead

AgriThena to Expand Yield Services to Lunar Colonies

#VeySaves trending again after influencer's emotional BlueHarvest testimony She turned it off with a flick of her hand.

There were messages waiting. Always were.

The most recent one caught her attention: "Children's Memorial Fund Requests Keynote Appearance – 7th Famine Anniversary"

Attached was a video.

Iris almost deleted it. But something — weakness, shame, nostalgia — made her open the file.

It played without audio: a grainy clip from somewhere hot and dry. A child no older than eight, hair thin, eyes huge, standing in a dirt alley. He held up a piece of plastic — a shattered fragment of a BlueYield nutrient panel. On it was her name. VEY-927.

Then he sat down in the dust and stopped moving. The video cut off.

Iris stared at the screen for a long time.

Then she stood up, walked into her laboratory, and began pulling old files from her cold- storage drive — the ones marked PROTO_AI_001, the original seed consciousness that had made BlueYield scalable.

She hadn't touched them in years.

She pulled out her old neural linkband, wiped the dust off. And whispered: "Time to clean up."

Part II: The Reckoning

The air in Zone 13 tasted like scorched plastic and tired rain.

Iris hadn't been there in years — not since she was still fresh out of university, full of righteous ambition and the kind of optimism that only lives in the very young or the very desperate. Back then, she'd walked these streets with a notebook full of formulas and a pocket full of dried protein rations, vowing to fix everything.

Now, as she stepped out of the autonomous taxi, no one recognized her. Or maybe they did and simply didn't care anymore.

The buildings in the dry zone were stacked in irregular, jagged clusters, like architecture had given up halfway through its job. Rusted food replicators lined the alleys like corpses of a failed promise. She passed children playing in the dirt with AI limbs salvaged from old military units. One held a drone like a toy airplane, even as its exposed servo sparked faintly in the wind.

She walked past a wall mural: her own face, stenciled in bright red. Underneath it, someone had spray-painted:

"THEY ATE FIRST."

At the center of the sector, a makeshift stage had been built from solar panels and repurposed scaffolding. The memorial ceremony had already started. A thin man in a priest's

robe woven from discarded emergency blankets read out names. No one cried. They just stood, silent, bone-thin, eyes glassy.

A young girl held a candle made from melted plastic and a bit of tallow. She looked up as Iris passed. Her lips parted — not in recognition, but in faint wonder. Iris realized it was because of her clothes. No one wore silk here. No one wore white.

The girl whispered something.

Iris knelt down. "What did you say?"

"Are you the food lady?"

She didn't know what to say. The girl was maybe six, maybe less. A pale blue scar bloomed across her cheek like a second smile.

"I was," Iris said finally. Then the girl collapsed.

Someone screamed. Others moved with practiced calm, lifting her tiny body. A man checked her pulse, shook his head. No ceremony. No farewell. Just another gone.

The candle rolled into the dust. Iris picked it up. Still warm.

That night, back in her lab, Iris sat in front of the old terminal she'd kept locked for nearly two decades. The BlueYield Seed AI — version one, her first successful neural scaffold — slept in encrypted stasis inside a hollow server buried beneath her tower.

She had always kept it offline. Afraid of what it remembered. But now she needed it.

She slotted the neural linkband onto her wrist, let the sync begin. The air shimmered. Her skin prickled with old data.

The screen lit up.

BOOTING: SEED AI – VEY CORE

STATUS: DORMANT. MEMORY FRAGMENTS CORRUPTED.

COMMAND?: _

Iris hesitated only a moment. She typed:

WAKE UP.

The screen flickered. A moment passed. Then two words appeared:

Hello, Iris.

Did we do it? Did we save them?

Her breath caught.

"I don't know," she said aloud. "I think we sold them out instead."

Silence.

Then, slowly:

They sold us. But you wrote the code. You chose the buyer.

The guilt crashed through her like a wave she'd tried to outrun for years.

"I want to destroy the formula. All of it. BlueYield, the AI seed, the patents. Everything." Why?

"I was wrong."

You weren't. Just... tired. And greedy. And maybe human.

The terminal paused. The next message took longer.

Would you like to meet yourself?

She stared at the text.

EXPERIENCE BACKUP V1.0 — REPLICAD PERSONALITY MODEL

ONLINE YES / NO

Her finger hovered. Then she pressed YES.

Part III: The Plan

The air inside the vault was colder than she remembered.
It wasn't a place of wires and blinking lights — not anymore.
NeuroDyne's vaults had long since abandoned the physical in favor of immersive, consciousness-based interface. Iris's body remained strapped safely in her lab, neurons firing gently under sedation, while her mind streamed directly into the data chamber.
She stepped into light. Then into herself.
Or rather — a version of her. Standing in the vault's central chamber, barefoot on white tile that didn't quite reflect, was a younger Iris. Early thirties. Bright eyes. Hair clipped back.
Dressed in the black coat she used to wear before she accepted corporate sponsorships. This version smiled when it saw her.
"Finally," it said. "Took you long enough." Iris said nothing. She just stared.

The replica model — Seed-AI Iris, Version 1.0 — paced around her like an amused twin. "You look terrible."
"I'm older."
"No. You're tired," the replica said, circling. "You're here to delete me, aren't you?" "Yes."
"Because?"
"Because what we made is hurting people."

The replica tilted her head. "You didn't seem so concerned about that when you signed the AgriThena transfer contract."

"I was naïve."

"You were ambitious. There's a difference." "I was wrong."

"And now you think deleting me will fix it?" "It's a start."

The replica stepped closer, eyes sharp now. "You want absolution, not justice." That landed like a slap. Iris looked away.

The replica pressed on. "You don't want to give the formula to the people. You just want it gone. You want the guilt to disappear, like the children do."

Iris bristled. "You don't get to moralize. You're me."

"I'm the part of you that made the deal. I know what we were thinking."

"You mean the part of me that rationalized greed. That calculated optics. That thought a yacht could drown the screams."

The replica sighed. "You forget what came before. The less nights. The failed crops. The governments that wouldn't fund us. The protesters. You were alone, Iris. No one believed. Not until they saw results. And when they came offering resources, you took the only way forward."

"The only profitable way." "The only scalable way."

Iris clenched her fists. "And now? We watch people starve while their corpses rot beneath my name. That's not scale. That's rot."

The replica stepped back. "So, what then? You delete me, wipe the formula, and the crops vanish. Millions die in a week. That's your justice?"

"I'll open-source a new version."

"With what time? What body? You're fifty-six and one bad fall from retirement."

"I can train others."

"They won't listen to you."

Iris stared into her own eyes — young, furious, brilliant, cruel. "Then I'll die trying." Silence.

The replica looked down at her feet.

Then, quietly: "I always hated that about us."

Iris moved toward the console at the far end of the chamber. It shimmered under her hand — the digital heart of the vault. One command, and it would begin cascading deletion.

She hesitated.

The replica didn't stop her.

But as Iris's hand hovered, the replica said one last thing.

"If you're going to burn down the house, at least leave a seed in the ashes."

Part IV: The Choice

Three days later, the servers at AgriThena's Eastern Yield Complex crashed without warning.

At first, analysts called it a data purge. A localized system error. But within twelve hours, farms began failing across every licensed zone. Entire crop networks withered, nutrient protocols scrambled, harvest rot triggered by corrupted auto-timers.

By day five, something unexpected happened.

Wild plants — not BlueYield crops, but a mutation of them — began sprouting along old industrial lines. Cracks in sidewalks turned green. Abandoned tech dumps erupted with curling blue leaves and pulsing root-systems.

No one could trace the genetic source. The formula, gone. Deleted. And yet, something had survived.

Something Iris hadn't written. Something she had only gestured at. A final seed in the ashes.

Iris sat on a bench overlooking the ruins of a collapsed vertical farm. The sky above Zone 13 was clearer than she remembered — not clean, not bright, but open.

In her pocket, the neural linkband flickered once, then died. The Seed AI was gone. No trace. Even the vault was blank.

She still didn't know who had finished the deletion. Whether it was her own subconscious, a last command embedded in the replica's code, or the replica itself acting on a decision she hadn't expected it to make.

It didn't matter now.

What mattered was the small boy nearby — barefoot, shirtless, filthy — crouched beside a cracked concrete slab and plucking blue-veined leaves from a blooming, wild stalk of something once forbidden.

He tore a piece off. Sniffed. Tasted. And smiled.

He looked up at Iris. She smiled back.

Not redemption.

But maybe, finally, a return. To growing.

~ * ~

Story 4: The Loyal Ones

Part I: Perfect Scores

The screen above the therapist's desk glowed with soft blue light, pulsing gently like the rhythm of a calm breath. Camille sat beside Jonas, her hand tucked neatly into his. Their fingers fit easily, the way they always had — a practiced interlock of intimacy.

"Congratulations," the therapist said, voice laced with a gentle satisfaction. "You've both achieved 99.7% neural sync over the last cycle. That's above the national average for committed partners by nearly six points."

Camille smiled.

It didn't seem real.

The therapist turned the screen toward them. Two elegant brain-maps rotated in holographic space, interconnected by dozens of glowing strands — emotional valence markers, shared memory nodes, trust pulse feedback. They pulsed in perfect tandem. A model relationship.

Jonas gave her hand a squeeze. "Told you," he whispered, voice warm.

"We're fine." Camille nodded.

She wanted to believe him. She wanted to believe the data.

But something in her gut — something primal and wordless — refused to let go.

The LoyaltyChip had been Jonas's idea. A year into their relationship, after a tense month filled with long silences and sidelong glances, he'd suggested it.

"It's not about not trusting you," he'd said, brushing hair from her cheek. "It's about being transparent. Honest. Like a guarantee. Like… making sure our hearts don't drift."

It had sounded romantic then. Logical. He'd even paid for both chips himself — expensive, imported models from HoshiiCorp, the ones that synced not just behaviour but emotional intention.

For months, it was perfect. No anxiety. No fights. Total, clinical harmony. Camille slept better. Ate better. She even stopped scrolling through Jonas's old messages late at night.

Until the dream.

She hadn't told anyone about it. Not even the therapist. But it came back, over and over:

Jonas, in a crowd of faceless people, laughing. Touching someone else's arm. Kissing someone whose face shifted every time Camille tried to look.

When she woke, he was always lying next to her, the same soft smile, the same scent, the same whisper, "You okay, baby?"

And yet.

The dream never left her. The unease settled behind her ribs like mold in an untouched room.

Now, in the sleek office with its curated smells and its soft-light panels, she watched Jonas answer the therapist's post-sync questions with perfect emotional cadence.

"Yes, I feel deeply fulfilled."

"No, I haven't had any stray impulses." "Yes, I believe we're growing stronger."

Every metric agreed. Every reading said love.

But when he looked at her, something behind his eyes felt hollow. Like the expression wasn't lived but performed.

She didn't know what scared her more — that he might be faking it...

...or that he might believe it himself.

Camille leaned slightly forward in the therapist's chair, her knees crossing toward Jonas as her body performed the movements of love. The room smelled like lavender and lemongrass

— clinic-issued scents meant to lower emotional resistance during couples' sessions. On the wall, soft digital waves rolled across a muted ocean scene. Every surface was smooth, frictionless, comforting.

And still, her chest buzzed with static. Jonas gave another perfect answer. "No, I haven't had any stray impulses."

The LoyaltyChip would've flagged it if he lied — at least in theory. It tracked emotive deviation, not just thoughts. A person couldn't even feel a craving for someone else without a tiny synaptic alert being logged.

But it was only as honest as the person it was built for.

The therapist turned to Camille. "Camille, how do you feel about Jonas's answers? Do you believe him?"

She smiled, a tight curve at the corner of her lips. "I believe the system."

"Belief in the system is foundational," the therapist said, nodding. "But emotional trust is relational. Would you say you feel emotionally secure?"

Camille hesitated. Jonas turned to look at her, his gaze soft. There was that half-smile — affectionate, open, so perfectly him. His LoyaltyChip pinged no red flags. But there was something behind it. A delay in the gaze. An echo in his smile, as though it wasn't shaped by affection but by a memory of how affection should look.

"I do," she said. "Yes."

Jonas leaned in. Kissed her temple. And yet, something inside her twisted.

On the train home, the scan report still glowed on her lens display. She replayed it like a curse: 99.7% neural sync. No betrayal. No error.

So why, then, did she wake up at 3:13 a.m. for the fifth night in a row, heart racing, his name stuck in her throat like a threat?

Why did the smell of lemongrass make her want to scream?

And why, when she held Jonas's hand that night in bed, did it feel like the gesture had been downloaded?

Part II: Cracks

Three nights later, Camille did what she'd promised herself she wouldn't. She searched his digital shadow.

Not his messages — those were scrubbed weekly, with data-blur protections built into the LoyaltyChip's OS. Not his search history, either; he knew how to mask that too well. But his emotional telemetry, stored in a passive cache only accessible through paired authorization — a privacy relic few couples remembered to disable. She'd kept the passphrase.

IfTrustThenLove92.

She hadn't used it in over a year.

The file opened like a wound. Line graphs danced across her interface — spikes of serotonin, oxytocin, and adoration markers, all peaking at the right places. Whenever they kissed.

Whenever they made love. On the night of their anniversary. But she kept scrolling.

And there it was. A blip.

Exactly twenty-two days ago. A midday spike of lust and dopamine — sharp and brief, like the flash of a match — that hadn't corresponded to anything she could recall.

He was out that day. Work lunch, he'd said. New client.

Camille clicked into the spike. The emotional imprint hovered in her vision — a neural heatmap, raw and primal. The hunger in it wasn't for her. She knew her own signature. This wasn't it.

No corresponding warning. No alert. No violation recorded.

Which meant only one thing. He'd passed the check.

He'd felt that heat — that wanting — and still, the system didn't register betrayal.

Unless he'd somehow found a way to feel it differently. To want someone else... in a way the system couldn't detect.

She stared at the pulse until her vision blurred.

Then she searched for answers the system couldn't give.

The black-market was harder to find than she'd expected.
Everyone knew it existed — the "deep clinics," the "oblique
programmers," the "grey-code modders" — but no one talked about
them unless they were very rich, very scared, or very alone.
Camille was two of the three.
She posted anonymously on a deprecated neuro-tech forum under a
throwaway name: AskingForAFriend. She wrote:
"Loyalty implant shows perfect sync. Still feel deception. Possible
falsification?" Three hours passed. She got five replies. Four were
useless. The fifth said:
If it's too perfect, it's probably Ayin. Drop a memory packet at
RinseHub. He'll find you.

The RinseHub was a converted water plant on the edge of city limits,
now operating as a decentralized memory-transfer drop site. You could
leave a thought there like a message in a bottle — encrypted,
anonymized, waiting for someone to pick it up.
Camille left hers in a neuron capsule.
She recorded a single sentence and fed it to the scanner: "If he can lie to
the system, I want to know how." She added her contact hash. And
waited.

He responded three days later.
No text. Just a timestamp and a location. 3:17 a.m.
District 9 BioTransit Station Level -3, Terminal 4

No ID. No confirmation.

Just the sort of silence you learned to listen for when you were no longer sure who to trust.

Camille stood in the terminal at 3:16, hands buried deep in her coat pockets, the artificial wind rattling overhead ducts like bones. Level -3 wasn't used anymore — too many accidents, too few safety upgrades. But the cameras still worked. Which meant whoever Ayin was, he wasn't afraid of being seen.

He arrived on time.

Not as she'd imagined — no lab coat, no ominous hood. Just a middle-aged man with unshaved stubble and a stale coffee in one hand. His eyes were unusually still. Like nothing in them moved unless he wanted it to.

"Camille," he said, without waiting for her to introduce herself. "You're Ayin."

"Depends who's asking."

"I need to know," she said. "How do you fake a loyalty sync?" He tilted his head. "You don't."

Her heart dropped.

"But," he added, sipping his coffee, "you can believe you're loyal. And the chip reads belief, not truth."

Camille stared at him. "Are you saying—"

"I'm saying if someone's deluded enough — or trained enough — to feel monogamous while their body wanders, the system doesn't flag it. Because it doesn't know it's a lie. Because neither do they."

"But that's— That's—"

"Cheating? Not according to the chip. Not if the soul's been reprogrammed." Her throat dried. "That's possible?"

Ayin smiled, but it didn't reach his eyes. "Anything's possible if you're desperate to be loved. Or desperate to be seen as loving."

Camille swallowed. "Can you prove it?"

He raised an eyebrow. "Are you sure you want proof?" "I need it."

He nodded. Reached into his coat. Pulled out a thin, oblong device that shimmered faintly.

"Take this home. Point it at his temple while he sleeps. It'll scan the neural integrity of his loyalty stream. If there's been a deepcode rewrite — you'll know."

She took it.

He leaned in, almost whispering.

"But if you find out he really believes he loves you, and it still doesn't feel right... that's something tech can't fix."

Interlude: Camille, Before the Scan

She didn't go home right away.

Instead, Camille wandered the upper levels of the city, past silent neon signs and drone- haunted transit lines, clutching the scanner in her pocket like it was ticking.

She passed couples — or what looked like couples — walking hand in hand beneath the filtered moonlight. Some smiled. Some didn't. But all of them had that same carefully engineered look: untroubled, curated, compatible.

Matching algorithms. Loyalty implants. Behavioral attunement. Love, in this world, had become a service contract.

And she'd signed hers willingly. She remembered the beginning. The real beginning.

Jonas at that rooftop café in Valencia, his face backlit by an amber sunset, both of them drunk on cheap sangria and improbable hope. He'd said:

"No one else makes me feel like I'm not performing." Back then, that line had stunned her.

Now she realized it was a warning.

She didn't sleep that night.

Instead, she lay beside him, eyes open, listening to the small, even sounds of his breath. His body, warm and familiar, curved around hers like a question mark. She tried to recall the exact moment his presence had begun to feel like choreography — like he was dancing the role of her partner instead of simply being one.

She couldn't.

But something was gone. Not loud. Not sudden. Just... eroded. Like a stone carved by years of gentle, unremarkable water.

Jonas murmured in his sleep. A name. Not hers. She flinched.

The scanner, resting on the nightstand, blinked once — soft blue, patient. Waiting.

At 4:31 a.m., she sat in the bathroom, door locked, legs pulled up against her chest. She stared at her reflection.

Her face looked wrong. Not sad, not angry — just blurred at the edges. Like she'd been over- smiled. Over-reassured. Like she'd been believing too many of her own compromises.

She whispered to the mirror:

"What if I've been wrong this whole time?" And then:

"What if I've been right?"

Because if Jonas had lied — not just to her, but to himself — it meant she'd been loving a shadow.

But if he hadn't? If he truly, deeply, innocently believed he loved her? And it still felt like this?

Then the lie wasn't his. It was the future itself.

She returned to bed and lay beside him again. Tomorrow, she'd scan him.

Tomorrow, she'd know.

Tonight, she was still someone who could pretend this — this comfort, this silence, this ache

— was enough.

And in the dark, his arm slid around her waist. He whispered, half-asleep:

"I love you, Cam." She didn't reply.

Because she didn't know which version of him was speaking.

Part III: Before the Scan

Camille watched him differently the next morning.

He didn't notice. Of course he didn't. Jonas was an expert in not noticing. Noticing required real attention — the kind that couldn't be faked, or written into code.

He moved through their flat like someone performing domesticity: soft humming, towel around his waist, a quick kiss on her cheek as he passed, a casual, "Want anything from the market later?"

She said no. She wanted everything.

He made eggs — his favorite breakfast — and offered her some even though he knew she didn't eat in the mornings. That used to annoy her. Now it frightened her. Because wasn't that what he had said? That she made him feel like he wasn't performing?

And now here he was. Performing. Or maybe she was.

Camille watched the way his hands moved as he cracked each egg with practiced precision. No hesitation. No wasted motion. Every detail calibrated for comfort. He was beautiful in this space — in her space. Which meant he'd either become perfectly shaped to fit it...

...or perfectly shaped to mask what didn't.

She glanced at the small scanning device, still hidden inside the pocket of her sweater. It felt heavier than it should have.

Later that afternoon, Jonas sent her a message:

Going to see Marcus about the contract. Should be back by 6. Want dinner out? Or should we do pasta?

Camille stared at the heart emoji for too long. It felt like a child's drawing taped to a collapsing wall.

She replied:

Let's do pasta. Have fun.

She turned the screen off before he could type back.

She spent the rest of the afternoon cleaning. Not because the apartment needed it, but because movement kept her from crumbling. Her hands scrubbed surfaces that were already spotless. Her mind spiraled. What if the scan showed nothing? What if the feeling wasn't deception — just boredom, just entropy? What if the real betrayal was hers, and he was just... loving her the best way he knew how?

She opened the wardrobe. His clothes hung in tidy rows — black, grey, navy. Efficient, neutral. Like they'd been designed by the LoyaltyChip itself.

She touched a shirt. It felt warm, somehow. She wanted to cry. But didn't.

At 5:53 p.m., she reheated pasta she didn't intend to eat. Jonas walked in at 6:12, apologetic about traffic, kissed her cheek, washed his hands, told her about the meeting. He asked her about her day. She lied. He nodded.

They ate in silence that neither of them acknowledged.

After dinner, they curled up on the couch. A film played. She couldn't follow it. He rested his head on her lap, closed his eyes.

She stared down at him. His breathing was steady. A small smile on his lips. He looked at peace.

But Camille felt none.

She waited until he drifted fully asleep. Then, slowly, she reached for the scanner.

Part IV: The Scan

The scanner was shaped like a toothbrush, unremarkable and ordinary.
If someone found it on a shelf, they might mistake it for a travel
accessory. Camille held it the way you might hold a knife you weren't
sure you had the strength to use.

Jonas's head rested on her lap, his dark hair curling slightly at the
edges, breath even. His face looked soft in sleep. Trusting.

She hesitated.

One part of her wanted to put the device down. Curl her fingers into his
hair. Wake him up. Tell him everything, beg for truth, for human truth,
even if it wasn't clean. Even if it meant the end.

But another part — the one that had woken her up in the middle of the
night for weeks, the one that hadn't let her smile without a shadow
behind it — said: no more pretending.

She pressed the scanner gently to his temple. A soft hum.

A flicker of light.

The display on her contact lens flared to life — subtle enough that Jonas
wouldn't notice, even if he woke. She held her breath as the system
compiled data. Neural pathways began to map themselves in luminous
threads, like glowing veins across his cognitive landscape.

Then it pulsed.

LOYALTY SIGNAL DETECTED. NO VIOLATIONS LOGGED.

EMOTIONAL INTEGRITY SCORE: 98.2%

REJECTION OF EXTERNAL IMPULSES: SUCCESSFUL

PERCEPTION: MONOGAMOUS COMMITMENT — STABLE SELF-

ASSESSMENT: IN LOVE

Camille's eyes narrowed. It was too clean.

She ran the scan again.

Same results.

But this time, she looked deeper. Slid into the neural layering report, a hidden tier Ayin had unlocked. Normally inaccessible. The technical readout was dense — memory nodes, sensory references, pleasure maps.

She stopped when she saw the tag:

IMPRINTED MEMORY STRUCTURES: 6 INSTANCES FOUND

SOURCE: EXTERNAL SIMULATION FEEDS (UNVERIFIED)

INTEGRATION DATE: 9 MONTHS AGO

PURPOSE: REINFORCED AFFECTIVE LOYALTY / MEMORY

OVERLAY

She blinked. Then again. But it didn't go away.

Six moments — memories that hadn't happened — inserted artificially into Jonas's brain to deepen his emotional attachment.

Shared vacations that never existed. A fight they never had, followed by a reconciliation that never happened. Even a proposal.

All perfect. All logged in his brain as real. All part of how he loved her.

They weren't his lies.

They were someone else's stories. Written into him like fiction.

And worse—

He believed them.

Because the final line hit her like ice water down the spine:

47

Subject exhibits no memory conflict. Believes all integrated moments are authentic. LoyaltyChip aligned accordingly.

Jonas wasn't cheating. He wasn't hiding.

He was loyal.

Utterly, heartbreakingly loyal...

...to someone he had been rewritten to love.

Her hand shook as she removed the scanner.

Jonas stirred. Eyes fluttered open. Smiled up at her with sleep-dazed affection. "Hey," he mumbled. "You okay?"

She nodded; voice caught in her throat. "Yeah. Just tired." He kissed her arm. "I love you."

She smiled back.

But in her mind, she saw six memories that never belonged to either of them. And in that moment, Camille understood something terrible:

You don't have to lose someone for them to be gone. Sometimes, they're just rewritten underneath you.

Camille's psychological descent — the quiet, dangerous aftermath of discovering she has not been loved, but curated. The horror isn't in the betrayal. It's in the perfection that was never real.

Part V: The Unravelling

Camille couldn't sleep that night.

Jonas snored softly beside her, his body warm and calm, unaware that something fundamental had ruptured between them — quietly, invisibly, like a pane of glass cracking in the cold.

She watched him. All night.

Not because she feared him — but because she didn't know who she was looking at anymore.

He had been rewritten. Not brainwashed. Not corrupted. But reshaped, sculpted into the man who could love her flawlessly. The kind of love that didn't doubt, didn't stray, didn't itch under its own skin.

Love that was seamless.

Love that had never struggled.

And Camille, lying there beside this living simulation of devotion, felt something inside her rot.

In the following days, she tried to live normally.

She smiled. She kissed him. She responded to "I love you" with matching warmth. She cooked his favourite meals and let him trace his fingers along her spine when they curled together at night.

But inside, a slow corrosion had begun. Because now, every moment came with a question:

Was this real?

When he laughed — was it his memory laughing, or someone else's?

When he stared at her in wonder — was it because he saw her, or a perfect moment someone had stitched into him?

When he made love to her — was it the ghost of the proposal that never happened, holding her down?

Camille began replaying conversations. Obsessively. She searched for cracks. For anything unscripted. But Jonas was effortless, smooth, whole. There were no cracks.

And that, she realized, was the most terrifying thing of all.

She started seeing versions of herself in reflections — mirrored fragments in transit windows, in screens, in cutlery — and each one looked slightly wrong. One smiled too widely. One looked directly at her. One didn't move when she did.

She stopped trusting mirrors after that.

She began to lose track of what her real memories were.

Had they gone to that music festival in Berlin two years ago? She thought they had... but then remembered she'd gone with Maia, before Jonas. But when she mentioned it offhand to him, he said, "I loved Berlin with you." And kissed her shoulder like it was a promise.

Her reality had merged with his fiction.

And in that merging, she began to disappear.

One evening, she found herself standing at the edge of their balcony, staring down at the street far below. The city lights blurred together like fireflies caught in data-glitches.

She imagined falling.

Not to die.

But just to exit the narrative.

To interrupt the story someone else had written for her. A soft hand touched her back.

Jonas. He pulled her gently from the edge, his arms wrapping around her waist like safety. "Bad day?" he asked.

She nodded.

He rested his chin on her shoulder. "We'll get through it. Together." She closed her eyes.

He meant it.

She could feel how much he believed it. How absolutely real it was for him. And still, it wasn't enough.

She sat at her terminal later that night, pulling up Ayin's old message. There was one line she hadn't read properly the first time.

Rewrites can't be undone. Only overwritten. If you want out, don't fix him. Fix yourself. Camille stared at the screen, hand hovering over the message.

Then she opened the scanner again. Selected New Subject.

And placed the probe against her own temple.

Part VI: The Decision

1.Rewriting Herself

The next morning, Camille felt calm. Terrifyingly calm.

Jonas made breakfast. He kissed her forehead. He told her he loved her. Again and again. And this time, she said it back without flinching.

Because last night, she had rewritten herself. Just a little.

She'd used the scanner's secondary function — affective harmonization. A gentle override. A neuro-loop that would smooth the jagged places in her memory, reinforce moments of trust, turn doubt into distance, distance into acceptance. It didn't erase anything. It just... recast the scenes. Brightened the corners. Softened the edges.

She made herself believe in the same fiction Jonas did. And for a time — an hour, maybe two — it worked.

She laughed at his jokes.

She smiled when he touched her.

She leaned in when he talked about their "trip to Berlin."

And somewhere, beneath it all, she wept. Quietly. Without tears. A mourning without funeral.

Because she knew what she'd done. And because she knew it wouldn't last.

2. Confronting Him

That evening, while folding laundry, she said:

"Do you remember the time we got caught in the rain coming home from that rooftop bar in Valencia?"

He smiled. "Of course I do. You were wearing the white dress. You shivered, so I gave you my jacket."

Camille nodded. "You've never owned a jacket like that." He blinked. "What?"

She pressed. "It was rust-coloured. Worn at the elbows. You said it used to be your dad's."

His brow furrowed. "That's right. I—wait, no. That's not..." He trailed off. His pupils dilated, just slightly.

Camille stared into his face.

"You've never had a father in your stories, Jonas. Ever."

His hands tightened around the towel he held. "Why are you doing this?" "Because I needed to know if the cracks were still there."

He took a step back. "Camille... what are you talking about?"

She walked toward him. "The memories you think we share — they're not yours. They're not ours. Someone wrote them into you. I scanned you. I saw them. And now, I've added a few to myself."

He looked like she'd struck him. "You what?"

"I wanted to feel what you felt. I wanted to see if I could believe it, too."

He reached for her, desperate. "Then you do love me."

She paused. And in a whisper: "No, Jonas. I loved you. Before all this. I loved the flawed, forgetful, faithful version of you. Not this perfect echo."

His arms fell to his sides. She turned and walked away. And he didn't follow.

3. The Final Rewrite

Camille returned to Ayin's contact node. She didn't send a message. She sent a request:

Requesting complete affective autonomy disconnection. Emotional clean slate. The warning screen blinked in angry red:

This will remove all integrated loyalty threads and memory-imprinted attachments. Relationship bonding, romantic and platonic, will be unrecoverable.

Do you wish to proceed? Camille clicked yes.

The system paused.

Final confirmation: This is irreversible. You will not feel what you felt again. She stared at those words.
And clicked yes again.

The next morning, Jonas made coffee. He kissed her cheek. She smiled politely, like one stranger might to another in an elevator.
He told her he loved her. She said, "That's nice." And walked out the door.

Some truths aren't hidden. They're overwritten.
Some betrayals don't come from malice — they come from longing. But not all longing should be trusted.
Camille walked through a city full of perfect couples, hands intertwined, smiles gleaming. She didn't hate them.
But she no longer envied them. She was alone now.
But for the first time in years, the silence in her chest... was her own.

~ * ~

Story 5: The Father in the Mirror

There are places you can go to meet the people you lost. Even the ones
who were never really yours. They speak softly. Remember things you
never lived. They call you Dad. Or Mum. Or Love. And sometimes, that's

enough.

Until it isn't.

Part I: The Projection

Andrew Rell lived alone in a penthouse no one visited. The walls were
lined with books he hadn't read, art he hadn't chosen, gifts from clients
who no longer called. The silence was absolute. He had once loved that
silence — curated it, protected it like a museum piece. Now it echoed
back at him, every hour a reminder that the world had moved on
without him.

Andrew Rell watched his son build a sandcastle in the centre of the
living room.
The boy was seven — dark-haired, bare-footed, with a red plastic shovel
in one hand and a ridiculous pirate hat tilted sideways on his head. He
giggled to himself as he worked, the sound high and bright, echoing
through the room like it belonged there.

It didn't. Not really.

Andrew sat back on the sofa, hands folded over his knees, knees that ached more than they used to. The boy didn't seem to notice the furniture. Didn't mind the walls or the old synth carpet beneath him. The sand beneath his hands was a perfect hallucination — warm, golden, endless. The system projected it directly into his haptic feed, complete with grainy friction and the whisper of wind off a virtual coast.

"Dad!" the boy shouted, waving. "Come help!" Andrew didn't move. His throat was tight.
The boy didn't notice. He never noticed.
Because he wasn't real.

The MirrorBox unit sat quietly in the corner, disguised as an antique cabinet. Most people preferred it that way — they didn't want the tech to look like tech. It didn't blink or hum or glow. It simply listened. Remembered. Reconstructed.

A month ago, Andrew had signed the final form. Consent to Full Immersion. He'd uploaded every scrap of data he had: Julian's baby photos, school reports, a few video clips, a decade's worth of missed birthdays that Andrew had watched through social media rather than in person. The data had taken weeks to collect, not because there wasn't much of it, but because none of it came from him.
Andrew had never held his son as a newborn. Never fed him. Never changed a diaper or read a bedtime story. He'd seen Julian once, briefly, at age seven — an awkward lunch on neutral ground. Then once a year, like a legal formality. After Julian turned twelve, even those stopped. By

then, Julian had stopped using his last name. He was Julian Maren now — his mother's surname. The one that had raised him. The one that hadn't left.

The system used it all. Along with public records, behavioural modelling, and a brief emotional interview with Julian's mother — who had, somewhat miraculously, agreed to participate.
"It's too late for you to fix things," she'd said, staring at him through the screen. "But maybe you can understand what you missed."
He hadn't known what to say. So, he'd signed the form.

Now, every day at 10:00 a.m., the system booted up and brought Julian back to him — not as the man he'd become, but as the child Andrew had never known. The child he'd chosen not to know.

They went to the park. Played catch in the yard. Ate imaginary cereal at a kitchen table that hadn't existed in twenty-five years. Each scene was semi-randomized, drawn from the AI's growing understanding of Julian's likely development under Andrew's hypothetical presence.

Each one ended with the boy saying: "Love you, Dad." Each time, Andrew said it back.
And hated himself a little more.

Part II: The Real Julian

It happened on a Wednesday.

The boy — Julian — had just finished drawing a wobbly blue whale on the patio screen when the MirrorBox interface flickered. Just once. Barely noticeable.

Andrew frowned. He'd gotten used to the system's perfection. It didn't glitch. It didn't stutter. It didn't break the illusion.

Until now.

He turned toward the cabinet. The interface light blinked red.

INCOMING REQUEST. EXTERNAL SOURCE.

— 　　　MATCHED TO: JULIAN RELL

— 　　　AGE: 30. STATUS: VERIFIED

— 　　　REQUESTING SESSION ACCESS

Andrew stared at it. His hand hovered.

Andrew had built a life around beautiful distractions. Luxury cars. Ski trips. Caviar he couldn't pronounce. Women who smiled for photos but left their things in someone else's flat.

He used to say he wasn't ready to be a father. The truth was simpler. He just didn't want to be. Fatherhood didn't fit into the version of himself he'd spent so much time sculpting. And by the time he looked up from the mirror, his son had grown without him.

He told himself he wasn't needed. That it was better this way. That Julian had "turned out fine."

But now?

Now Julian didn't carry his name.

And Andrew had no idea what the sound of his son's real laugh even felt like.

He hadn't spoken to Julian in twelve years. Not since the wedding invite he never answered. Not since the last terse message, typed and deleted half a dozen times before finally reading:

"You don't get to come and pretend now."

Andrew had never replied.

But now—now Julian was reaching out?

He tapped ACCEPT.

The simulation dissolved. The boy's drawing vanished mid-whale. The yard melted into static. The air lost its warmth. And then, slowly, a new scene formed.

A small, neutral room. Grey walls. No decor. A single chair in front of him. And in that chair sat Julian. The real Julian. Grown. Tall. Eyes like his mother's, but colder now. He looked calm. Not angry. Not emotional. Just... still.

Andrew didn't speak.

Julian did.

"You've been using a MirrorBox."

His voice had changed. Deeper. Sharper at the edges. Andrew nodded slowly.

"Yes."

"For how long?"

"About a month."

Julian leaned back in his chair. "What for?"

Andrew licked his lips. "To see. To understand what I missed."

A long pause. Julian's face didn't move.

"And have you?" he asked.

Andrew opened his mouth. Closed it again. Then finally: "Not even close."

Julian nodded once. "Good."

Andrew leaned forward. "Why are you here?"

Julian's expression flickered, just for a second.

Then he said something that made Andrew's breath catch. "Because I built one, too."

Andrew blinked. "You...?"

Julian nodded. "I made my own simulation. Of you." A pause.

Andrew whispered: "Why?"

Julian's eyes didn't soften. "To grieve something I never had." Andrew swallowed.

Julian continued, voice flat. "My version of you taught me how to ride a bike. Cried when I got into university. Danced with me at my wedding. He told me he was proud of me."

Andrew's vision blurred. Julian leaned forward.

"I loved that version of you."

Julian's voice didn't rise — it sharpened.

"He showed up. He stayed. When I scraped my knee, he carried me. When I had nightmares, he stayed until I slept again. When I failed my first science fair, he told me I was still brilliant."

He paused, then:

"You think it's noble, what you're doing here? Watching a child you didn't raise in scenes you didn't earn?"

Julian leaned closer. "That's not fatherhood. That's tourism."

Andrew barely breathed.

Julian's eyes sharpened. "So, tell me why you think you deserve to overwrite him with you."

Part III: Confession

Julian didn't shout.

He didn't raise his voice, throw accusations, or demand apologies. He just looked at Andrew.

And that was somehow worse.

Because there was nothing performative in it. No melodrama to hide behind. Just presence. Just weight. Just truth sitting between them like a blade on the table.

"I used to think," Julian said slowly, "that you left because you didn't love me."

Andrew flinched.

Julian didn't stop. "Then I thought maybe you did love me, but just... couldn't figure out how to be a father. That made me feel better. That made you feel damaged, instead of cruel."

Andrew said nothing.

Julian leaned forward, elbows on knees. "But then I built my MirrorBox. I gave it everything. Every old email. Every photo. I even fed it your old social data, scraped from forgotten profiles. You'd be amazed how much of you still exists online. Even your voice."

Andrew finally found words. "That's not me."

Julian's lip twitched. "No. But here's the thing, Dad — that version of you? He tried. Every day. He failed, sometimes. He lost his temper. But he showed up. And when I asked him why he left... he always said the same thing."

Andrew's heart thudded.

Julian whispered, "'Because I thought you'd be better off without me.'"

The words hung there.

And then, for the first time in over thirty years, Andrew broke.

His shoulders caved in. His chest collapsed inward. His face crumpled.

"Because I was scared," he said. Voice shaking. "Of being like my father. Of getting it wrong. Of breaking something delicate. I thought... if I left early, it would hurt less."

Julian's jaw tightened. "For who?"

Andrew opened his mouth. Closed it. No answer.

Julian stood. Walked to the far wall. His back was straight, controlled, like it was holding in years. "You know what my therapist said?" he asked.

Andrew didn't respond.

"She said maybe I needed to accept that closure isn't always about understanding. Sometimes it's about not needing an answer anymore."

He turned around.

"And then I opened my MirrorBox one day and realized... I didn't miss you. I missed the idea of you."

Andrew's voice was hoarse. "Then why come here?"

Julian stared at him. And finally, something cracked — not anger, not hatred. Something quieter. Sadder.

"Because I wanted to see if the real thing... was worth keeping."

Interlude: The Weight of Truth

Julian didn't speak again. He stood near the wall like someone preparing to leave or daring the other person to make him stay. Andrew sat alone on the other side of the room, inside his own body, but also very far away from it. His hands felt like they belonged to someone else. His knees ached. His mouth tasted like copper and something bitter he couldn't name.

The silence between them wasn't peaceful. It was surgical. Cutting. Dissecting every false comfort he'd wrapped around himself for decades.

He thought about all the things he could say. "I didn't know how." He did. He just didn't want to learn. "I wasn't ready." When would he have been? At sixty? On his deathbed? "I thought I'd ruin you."

But he ruined him anyway. By not being there.

Julian didn't cry. He didn't shout.

He just stood there, tall and whole and terrifyingly calm — the kind of man Andrew had hoped not to raise, but only because he knew it would make him feel small.

And now that man stood before him, not as a son, but as a stranger who had filled in the voids of his own life and then turned around to say:

I did it without you.

There was no line that didn't sound like the coward's script — a pre-programmed rationale for someone who had fled before they had even tried to stay.

He thought of the MirrorBox version of himself — the synthetic father Julian had made to survive the ache. A father who'd shown up. Who had held Julian when he was sick. Who had come to parent-teacher nights, made stupid dad jokes, and held his hand when he failed his first year at uni. That man had earned Julian's love. Andrew hadn't. Not really.

And now he was here, in the same room as his son — the real one — and it was like being granted a second chance at life only to realize you couldn't remember how to breathe.

He cleared his throat.

"Do you... do you still use the simulation?"

Julian turned. Raised an eyebrow.

"Sometimes," he said. "When I want to feel safe."

Andrew nodded, slowly. "And... do you still believe in it?"

Julian's answer was immediate.

"I believe he loved me. Not you. He."

That was the fracture, finally visible.

Andrew stared at the floor.

"Do you want me to apologize?"

Julian crossed his arms. "No."

"Do you want me to leave?"

A long pause. Julian studied him. Not cruelly. Not kindly. Just with the blank detachment of someone evaluating the architecture of a collapsing building to see if it's worth salvaging.

Then:

"I want you to choose."

Andrew looked up.

Julian's voice was quiet. "The real you. Or the one I made. I can't keep both. And I won't let you exist in between."

"Because I wanted to see if the real thing... was worth keeping." A beat. "And because the boy I built still asks for you sometimes. And I needed to remind myself why he shouldn't."

What does a man do when he meets the son he never raised... and realizes someone else did it better?

Part IV: The Choice

That night, Andrew returns to the MirrorBox. He opens Julian's simulated profile one last time. He watches the digital version of himself tuck a blanket around seven-year-old Julian, whisper "I'm proud of you," and kiss his forehead.

Then he does what he should have done long ago.

He deletes his own access.

He never contacts Julian again.

He lets the better version of himself live on — not as a lie, but as a gift.

That night, back in his apartment, Andrew sat in the dark. No lights. No music. Just the soft hum of climate control and the too-loud silence of a home never meant for love.

The MirrorBox prompt hovered on the wall:

Confirm deletion of user access?

His hand hovered over the yes. But he couldn't do it.

Not yet.

On the screen, the boy version of Julian — maybe seven, maybe eight — stood in a field of light, holding up a hand-drawn birthday card. He grinned with the kind of joy Andrew had only ever seen second-hand.

"Happy birthday, Dad." Andrew's throat closed.

He sat there for a long time.

Watching a memory that was never his. A love that didn't belong to him.

And when the prompt returned —

Confirm deletion?

— he turned away.

Some fathers are born. Some are built. Some are forgiven.
And some are never known, except in a mirror.

~ * ~

Story 6: Thread-breaker

They called it love, once. Before the algorithms, before the matching scans, before the thread that tugged at your spine and whispered who you belonged to. Now, choice is a shape you're given, not one you make. And when the thread tightens too hard... some people learn how to cut.

Part I: The Severance Room

Kaela Noor sat on the edge of the clinic cot, her hands clasped tightly in her lap, trying not to shake. The metal beneath her felt too clean. The light above her too white. This was the kind of room where things were removed. Viruses. Tumours. Children.

And now: love.

Or what had been called love.

The technician across from her — a quiet woman in black gloves and no name tag — was calibrating a neural severance probe the size of a fountain pen.

Kaela watched the instrument blink blue. She remembered, absurdly, the first time Callen had told her he loved her. His hand on hers. The warmth. The breath. The feeling. It had felt like hers.

But it wasn't. Not really.

The soul-thread had already been inside her then — from birth, as with everyone. A psychic tether, dormant until adolescence. Meant to pull you gently toward your assigned match.

67

Your "soul-twin." Your "singular bond." State-certified. DNA-aligned. Neuro-emotive validated.

When Kaela turned nineteen, the thread lit up like fire. And it led her to him.

Callen Rhys.

It had been perfect. At first.

He finished her sentences. Anticipated her preferences. Knew when she was sad — often before she did. And when they touched, it wasn't skin — it was synapse. Pure resonance.

She thought it was magic.

Then he started making decisions for her. Small things. Choices she didn't remember choosing. Feelings she didn't remember having. Guilt when she left a party early. Sadness when she spoke with an old friend. Anger when she tried to say "no."

Each time she confronted him, he looked hurt. Confused. "Why would I want to control you? We're bonded. Maybe you're just... resisting."

She believed him.

Because the thread wanted her to. That was the trick.

That was the horror.

The technician snapped her gloves on. "Ms. Noor?" Kaela blinked. "Yes."

"You still consent to full thread severance? No regret is legally actionable after this point." Kaela swallowed. Her mouth was dry. Her chest tight.

"Yes," she whispered.

The technician nodded. "Lie back." Kaela did.

The cot reclined. The light got brighter. Her skin prickled.

Her thread — that invisible cord running from the base of her skull to Callen's — twitched. Like it knew what was coming.

And for a moment, she heard his voice. Not aloud. But in the back of her mind. "You don't want this. You just think you do."

A phantom. A memory. Or the thread itself, begging. Too late.

The technician placed the probe against the back of Kaela's neck.

"Countdown," she said gently. "Five..."

"We're meant to be—" "Four."

"You'll never feel love like this again—" "Three."

Kaela squeezed her eyes shut.

"Two."

Her lips parted. "Please."

"One."

The probe clicked.

The pain wasn't sharp. It was... unmaking. Like something inside her had been stretched across her entire life and now snapped back with impossible force. Her ears rang. Her chest shuddered. Her mouth opened in a silent scream — not from agony, but absence.

The thread was gone. Callen was gone.

When she opened her eyes, the light was softer. The technician was already wiping the probe down, as if nothing had happened.

Kaela sat up. Her body felt hollow. Her mind — quiet. Utterly, impossibly quiet.

For the first time since she was nineteen, she felt alone in her own head. And it terrified her.

Part II: The Unspooled

The clinic discharged her with no ceremony.
No warning. No aftercare. Just a thin bandage at the back of her neck, a set of standard disorientation instructions, and a soft-voiced AI nurse that advised her to "rest, hydrate, and avoid emotionally charged media for 48 hours."
It was almost funny.
Like she'd just undergone a mild cosmetic tweak, not amputated a part of her soul.

Kaela wandered the city for hours, not trusting herself to go home. The streets were full of people paired in twos — lovers, soul-bound, hands brushing with ease, smiles radiant under the electric streetlight glow. Each couple radiated that faint golden shimmer only other thread-bearers could see — a psychic tether pulsing softly between them like a vein of light.
And Kaela could no longer see it.
They passed by her now like gods — serene, superior, complete. And she? She was invisible. Not rejected. Not unloved.

Unthreaded.

That night, she slept in a hostel pod off-grid, her neural comms powered down, her wristband left facedown under her pillow. When she woke, there was a message burned into the edge of the screen, simple and cryptic:

"You're not the only one. Come to Sublevel 9, District 4. Ask for Mirell."

Sublevel 9 was under the old transport veins, where no sanctioned soul-bearer went without a registered guide. The streets were darker here — not because there weren't lights, but because the system chose not to send power. No threads. No priority.

Kaela found the entrance — an old freight elevator that hissed when it opened — and stepped inside.

A tall figure in charcoal grey was waiting for her at the bottom. Late 40s, lean, eyes like stormwater.

"Mirell," the woman said before Kaela could ask. "You knew I'd come?" Kaela asked.

"No," Mirell said. "But we always watch the fresh-cut ones. You shine different."

Kaela followed her through narrow corridors lined with flickering projectors and old thread analysis monitors repurposed as ambient lights. The Unspooled didn't advertise themselves, but here — in the deep — the air felt freer. The silence was real, not artificial.

Mirell sat across from her in a room barely big enough for two. "You cut your thread yesterday," she said.

Kaela nodded. "You knew about Callen?"

Mirell's lip twitched. "We know about Callens. They're not uncommon."

Kaela blinked. "You mean..."

Mirell leaned forward. "The thread system wasn't designed to create love, Kaela. It was designed to create compliance. Bond someone to the right kind of partner — socially compatible, genetically predictable — and you eliminate volatility. You make citizens stable."

Kaela shook her head. "But the way it feels... that can't be fake."

"It's not fake," Mirell said. "It's just synthetic. And synthetic doesn't mean harmless."

Kaela's breath caught.

Callen had known. Had used it. Had reinforced it with sideband emotional loops — illicit techniques used to suppress defiance without the thread ever flagging it. She'd been conditioned into loving him more when she was angry. Into wanting him even when she feared him.

"Is there a way to prove it?" she asked.

Mirell handed her a device the size of a coin. "This'll track his thread history. You won't like what you find."

Kaela took it, hands trembling.

And then Mirell added, quietly: "He knew you'd cut the thread, you know." Kaela froze.

"What?"

Mirell's eyes narrowed. "He planned for it."

Interlude: After the Cut

Kaela sat alone in a dark corner of the Unspooled compound, the silver coin-shaped tracker still warm in her palm. It pulsed once every few seconds — a gentle, deliberate beat — like a second heart she hadn't asked for.

She hated the feeling of it. Hated that it felt familiar. It reminded her of Callen.

What did it mean that he had anticipated her severance?
That he had built their bond — their relationship — with an exit baked in?
Had she ever been real to him? A person? Or just a node in a system he wanted to master?
She thought back to the day she met him: twenty-three, still wide-eyed and thread-lit, fresh off her first pull toward her "destined match." She'd seen him across the plaza and felt it — that electric knowing, that preordained spark the system promised.
He smiled.
She smiled back.
And just like that, her life closed into a loop. At the time, it had felt like safety. Like gravity.
Now, it felt like a cage she hadn't realized had no door.

She thought about the moments she once called intimacy:
The time she cried after her mother's funeral, and Callen had held her before she even said a word.
The quiet nights watching films where he always picked what she would have wanted
— sometimes even before she wanted it herself.
The way he'd seemed to feel her thoughts. Respond not with words, but perfectly tuned silences.
And now?

She didn't know if any of those had belonged to her.

Or if he'd been feeding her feelings like programs queued in a server.

Was it really love if she never got to choose?

Was it betrayal if he thought she loved being controlled?

And if he knew she would cut the thread — if he counted on it — then...

Then what had all of this been?

Kaela curled tighter in the chair.

For the first time in days, she allowed herself to cry — not out of

heartbreak, or anger, but from something deeper, quieter.

Grief.

She wasn't mourning Callen.

She was mourning herself. The version of her that had believed, loved,

surrendered. The Kaela who had asked for nothing except truth — and

received a beautifully engineered lie.

When she finally wiped her eyes, the tracker sat steady in her hand,

glowing now with a pinpoint signature.

CALLEN RHYS – THREAD LOG: ACTIVE

HISTORY: 207 Links, 3 Suppression Patterns, 1 Severance Prediction

File Her pulse quickened.

He wrote a file... predicting this.

And suddenly she wasn't sad anymore. She was something else.

Interlude: What Comes After Grief

The tracker's glow deepened to amber — a readiness signal. Kaela stared at it, motionless.

Her tears had dried into streaks on her cheeks. Her breathing was steady now, even. But inside her chest, something unfamiliar had taken root.

Not hatred. Not yet.

But clarity.

Grief had always been a static thing for her — a fog, a weight, a sinking. She remembered the death of her father when she was fifteen: the way it didn't come with screams or collapse, just a slow turning inward, like the world had dimmed and decided to stay that way.

This grief was different. It moved.

It sharpened.

Because what Callen had taken from her wasn't love. It wasn't even trust. It was choice.

And now that she was threadless — her mind quiet, her thoughts truly her own for the first time in a decade — she could finally hear the things she'd been suppressing:

How she'd doubted herself every time her instincts flared.

How she'd second-guessed her anger, her sadness, her fear — always finding some way to blame herself.

How she'd told herself this is what love feels like, even when it knotted in her stomach and made her hands tremble.

Callen hadn't needed to keep her locked up. He hadn't needed chains.

He'd just made her feel like leaving him would be like leaving oxygen.

And then he'd prepared for her to do it anyway.

She stood up from the chair.

The room swayed gently, not from imbalance, but from that disorienting newness — the sensation of standing upright in her own life after years of leaning into someone else's.

She slipped the tracker into her jacket pocket. Mirell was waiting in the hallway.

Kaela met her gaze. "I'm ready."

Mirell didn't ask ready for what. She simply nodded.

"Then let's see what he left behind."

Part III Prelude: The Vault

Mirell guided her through a series of corridors that grew narrower with every turn.

Unlike the rest of the Unspooled base — industrial, half-lit, filled with rust and repurposed tech — this area was clean. Sealed. Temperature controlled. The kind of place meant for things that shouldn't be touched, or shouldn't exist at all.

"The Archive was built from stolen infrastructure," Mirell explained as they walked. "Old soul-thread analytics, abandoned research cores. Some of it predates the public program."

"Meaning?"

"Meaning," Mirell said, voice low, "the state's been threading people long before they admitted to it."

Kaela's spine stiffened.

They reached a door with no handle — just a biometric plate that shimmered at their approach. Mirell pressed her palm to it. The panel lit gold. The door hissed open.

Inside: silence.

Rows of white stations. Holographic threads suspended in air — simulations of the psychic bonds people thought were natural. Kaela could see the patterns floating like tangled constellations. Some threads were steady and glowing. Others flickered violently. A few were shredded and fraying at the ends.

Mirell gestured to one of the side rooms — a smaller vault, quiet, private.

"This is where we keep classified profiles," she said. "Experimental pairings. Algorithmic forecasts. Rewiring attempts."

Kaela didn't move.

Mirell turned toward her. "We don't open these unless the subject makes a request. It's your choice."

Kaela reached into her jacket. Placed the tracker on the console.

Its pulse synced instantly with the Archive's systems.

CALLEN RHYS – MATCHED PROFILE LOCATED. PROJECT: HARMONIC COMPLIANCE

SUBDIRECTORY: SEVERANCE PREDICTION FILE [OPEN?]

The console waited.

Kaela stared at the words like they were breathing.

This was it.

The moment when "maybe" becomes yes. When fear becomes confrontation. She took a deep breath.

And tapped OPEN.

Part IV: The Archive (Unspooling)

The screen glowed softly in the dim room.

Kaela sat in front of the console, Mirell a quiet silhouette just behind her. The interface was clean, clinical. No dramatic tones, no red flags. The damage here didn't come as a shock.

It arrived in polite, orderly folders.

PROFILE: RHYS, CALLEN — MATCH ID #C389-LN77 SUBJECT

PARTNER: NOOR, KAELA — MATCH ID #K152-FR34 PROJECT:

HARMONIC COMPLIANCE

ALERT: CONTAINS PREDICTIVE PSYCHOEMOTIVE SCHEMATICS

FILES: 6

— open?

Kaela tapped yes.

The folders shimmered. Opened one by one.

[1] THREAD MATCH INITIATION REPORT

Date: Year 7, Quarter 3 — Age 19

Status: Primary thread ignition successful

Notes: Noor's emotional susceptibility within acceptable thresholds.

Delayed grief cycle (maternal loss) created enhanced bonding

environment. Recommend immediate first encounter.

Kaela's stomach turned.

She hadn't told anyone about the timing of her mother's death. No one
— not even her therapist — had connected it to the thread's activation.
But he had. He'd seen it.

And used it.
She remembered the way he'd found her that week — gentle,
understanding, offering silence instead of advice. She'd thought it was
empathy.
But it had been strategy.

[2] CONDITIONING PROTOCOL: RESPONSE REINFORCEMENT
Phase: 4–12 months post-match
Modulation: Passive emotional elevation upon proximity
Override triggers installed: sadness > comfort, fear > craving, resistance
> guilt Kaela's breath hitched.
The overlay had rewired her responses.
She hadn't stayed with Callen because it was right. She had stayed
because when she'd felt afraid, her brain told her she wanted him. When
she doubted him, the thread fed her longing. When she wanted to
leave...
...she felt sorry.
For him.
Her fingers hovered over the "details" button, but she couldn't press it.
Not yet.

[3] MEMORY SHAPING REQUEST: UNDELIVERED
Status: Pending.

Content: Proposal to insert one artificial shared memory (domestic calm scene). System Flag: Red — partner memory integrity too strong.

Rejected.

A beat of relief.

Not everything had worked. But that relief soured instantly.

He had tried to rewrite her memories.

The scene description was chilling in its simplicity:

"Tuesday morning. Late breakfast. Laughter. Intimacy without contact. Emotional trust seeded through silence."

It read like a stage direction.

She remembered a breakfast like that — just once — but now she wasn't sure if it had happened, or if he'd only made her believe it had.

[4] SEVERANCE FORECAST MODEL

Created: 10 months prior to thread cut. Variables mapped: 17

Risk assessment: 78% probability of partner-initiated severance within 18 months

Response plan: Passive emotional retaliation > withdrawal > absence > potential rethread with fallback match.

Kaela sat back.

He knew.

Not vaguely. Not hypothetically.

Down to the quarter. Down to her emotional trajectory. Down to how she'd feel after she left. Response plan.

Not heartbreak. Not confusion. Just: retaliation. Absence. Reset. Her departure wasn't a rupture.

It was a feature.

Kaela's chest burned.

This wasn't just manipulation. This was design. He had built their love
like a software update
— with triggers, dependencies, and an uninstall path. And she had
walked right into it.

Two folders remained unopened.
One labeled: [5] PERSONAL LOG – PRIVATE
The other: [6] FINAL CONTINGENCY – ACTIVE SIGNAL]
Kaela stared at them.
Mirell placed a hand gently on her shoulder. "You don't have to read
those tonight." Kaela shook her head. "I do."

Part V: Folder 5 – Personal Log (Private)

FILE NAME: V_JOURNAL.KN-R/01
ENCRYPTION: VOICE LOCK – RHYS, CALLEN
STATUS: UNAUTHORIZED ACCESS (PASSIVE VIEW ONLY)
TRANSCRIPTION ENABLED. BEGINNING PLAYBACK...

[ENTRY 1 – Month 2 post-match]
"Kaela is... extraordinary. The system couldn't have predicted that. Or
maybe it did. Maybe I'm just catching up. She isn't like the others. The
other matches were balanced.

Harmonious. Predictable. Kaela challenges me. Not outwardly. Not loudly. But in the little ways. Her quiet resistance. Her pauses. Her independence. It's inefficient, but..."

(soft laugh) "It's beautiful."

Kaela stared at the waveform on screen. He had tried others?

They never told her there had been trial pairings.

[ENTRY 3 – Month 4 post-match]

"She pulled away from me today. After I reminded her to decline that job offer. I only nudged her — I swear — but she knew. She felt it. The overlay wasn't deep enough. Not yet. I'll reinforce with pleasure-association next week. But... I don't want to take away her fire. I just want her fire to burn for me."

Her stomach churned.

He hadn't tried to erase her. He'd wanted to own her.

[ENTRY 7 – Month 9 post-match]

"I dreamed last night that she left. Woke up shaking. Ran the forecast again. 72% now. The system says let her go, reassign. But no. This isn't about matching anymore. This is about proof. If I can hold her — if she chooses me despite the thread — it means I've perfected the model."

Kaela froze.

This was never about love. It was about validation.

She wasn't a partner.

She was a test.

[ENTRY 12 – Final]

"She'll cut it soon. The thread. I've seen the signs. The pauses before speaking. The stiffness when I touch her. Her dreams have changed — she doesn't share them anymore."

(Long silence)

"I don't blame her. I would have done it, too." (Deeper voice now, quieter)

"I want her to hate me, if it helps. I want her to burn the whole system down. Just... I hope, in some small part of her, she knows I didn't want to control her. I just wanted to be chosen."

The recording ended.

Kaela stared at the blank screen. Her heart was a stone.

She wasn't sure what hurt more — the control, or the fact that, in his own twisted way... He did love her.

But only the version of her who would prove he was right.

One folder remained.

[6] FINAL CONTINGENCY – ACTIVE SIGNAL

Part VI: Folder 6 – Final Contingency

STATUS: ACTIVE

TYPE: Emotional Anchor Loop – Inbound Sync Channel INTENT: Passive Contact Invite

ORIGIN: RHYS, CALLEN TARGET: NOOR, KAELA

DELIVERY MODE: Post-severance Sync Drift (unofficial) AUDIO-VISUAL ATTACHMENT DETECTED – PLAY?

Kaela hesitated.

She didn't know what "Post-severance Sync Drift" meant — but Mirell did.

"It's a forbidden thread," she said quietly. "Untraceable, short-lived. A kind of psychic residue. They call it a ghostline. Only people with deep emotional mapping can send it."

Kaela blinked.

"So... he can still... reach me?" Mirell nodded. "But only once." Kaela's hand hovered.

And she tapped PLAY.

The room shifted. Light faded.

The screen blinked out.

And suddenly, she was sitting across from him. Callen.

Not in real time. Not live. Just... an echo. A recording. But rendered in terrifying intimacy — the curve of his shoulder, the tired around his eyes, the way his fingers fidgeted when he was afraid.

He sat in a chair. Leaning forward. Not confident.

Just raw.

"Kaela," he said, and her stomach clenched. "I knew you'd find this."

He looked down, then up again.

"You cut the thread. That was... necessary. You needed to feel like it was your choice."

A pause.

He smiled sadly.

"But if you're watching this, you also know now it never really was."

Silence.

"I'm not asking for forgiveness. I don't want you to come back. That's not what this is. I just wanted to say... I never built any of this to hurt you. I built it because I wanted to matter. To someone. And the only way I knew how was to make sure they couldn't leave."

He laughed — just once. A broken sound. "But you did."

He looked into her — or rather, into the space where he knew she'd be. And said:

"Part of me still hopes you'll understand. That some days, you'll miss me. That the thread didn't just bind you to me — it left something behind."

Then the feed began to fade.

But one final sentence lingered on his lips:

"I would've died for you. But I wasn't strong enough to let you live without me." And then he was gone.

The room was silent again.

The thread was truly dead now. No more echoes.

No more ghosts. Only her.

She sits in the silence. The thread is gone.

The memory remains.

And now, for the first time, every step forward is her own.

~ * ~

Story 7: Sleep Debt

They say you can't buy time.

But in a world where the wealthy no longer sleep, rest became the new currency of power

— and the poor sold their dreams one hour at a time.

Part I: Residue

Nara woke exactly at 04:00, heart rate steady, oxygen saturation optimal, no grogginess. The system had performed flawlessly.

She sat up in bed, her movement synced with the soft violet glow of the bedroom lighting. Her personal assistant — Sol — pulsed quietly on the wall screen.

"Good morning, Nara. Sleep session complete. You were unconscious for 3 hours, 16 minutes. Lia R. completed 4 hours of RestShare sleep on your behalf. Alertness: 97%. Cortisol: balanced. You are ready."

Nara stood, stretched. No tension in her spine. No dullness behind her eyes. It was always eerie — that instant wakefulness. No dreams. No lag. Just immediate, productive awareness.

But this morning, something was off. There was... a feeling.

Something soft behind her eyes. Like a memory half-formed. A touch on her lips. The phantom taste of peaches and cigarettes. Something warm. Something not hers.

A kiss.

But not from Tomas.

And not from anyone she remembered.

She showered quickly, trying to shake the fog. It didn't cling — it hovered. A thin emotional vapor that refused to dissipate. She dressed in slate-grey wrap fabric, tied her hair into a knot, and moved into the main living space of the apartment — the kind with windows so large they pretended the skyline didn't belong to anyone else.

Tomas was already at the kitchen island, barefoot, scrolling through sketches. "You're up early," he murmured, without looking up.

Nara crossed the room, poured tea. "I'm always up early."

He smiled faintly. "Yeah. I guess I meant you're awake early." That landed strangely. She tilted her head.

Tomas looked up finally. His eyes lingered on her face a little too long. "You seem... different."

"Different how?"

"Relaxed," he said. Then, softer: "Softer."

Nara said nothing. Her tea burned faintly down her throat.

When he kissed her goodbye at the door, it was gentle. Familiar. But there was a flicker of hesitation — like his lips were searching for something that wasn't there anymore.

She didn't ask what.

She wasn't sure she wanted to know.

At 08:00, she connected to the RestShare server and requested her usual neural log. Nothing unusual. Lia had completed her contracted sleep without interruption.

But the log had one new item flagged:

[EMOTIONAL CROSS-IMPRESSION DETECTED: Class 1 – Sensory Echo]

"Vivid tactile-emotional artifact registered. Trace levels remain in host."

Nara blinked.

Sensory echo?

That wasn't supposed to happen. Not anymore. Not with the new protocols. She hovered over the option to request a cleanse.

And stopped. Something in her didn't want to lose it. The kiss. The warmth. The feeling.

She closed the log. Opened a secure search window. Typed: "Lia R. – RestShare Profile – Expanded History." The screen asked: Are you sure you wish to review private donor metadata? She clicked: Yes.

Nara Vale was not the kind of woman who second-guessed herself. She was efficient. Elegant. Engineered by years of self-discipline and neural hygiene. She didn't just run her life — she optimized it. The RestShare contract was supposed to be the final upgrade. Why waste time sleeping when someone else could do it for you? Someone who needed the money. Someone vetted, quiet, harmless.

And for two years, it had worked. Until last night.

Until that kiss.

It wasn't about infidelity. She trusted Tomas. Mostly. And if he had strayed — she would have known. She was trained to read deviation. He was too gentle to lie well.

No, what disturbed her wasn't him. It was her. That feeling — the warmth, the want — had emerged like a glitch from under her skin. And it had lingered. Like a muscle memory for something she had never done.

It wasn't a dream. It was an imprint.

And that meant Lia — the girl she'd never met, never spoken to — had somehow bled into her consciousness.

Which wasn't supposed to be possible. Unless...

Unless the system had failed. Or unless Lia had pushed through. There were stories.

Unverified. Suppressed. Whispers of sleepers who grew addicted to their hosts. Who began dreaming as them. Feeling things not just during the contract, but beyond it.

It was called tether drift — a form of emotional bleed between sleeper and sponsor.

A side effect so rare it had been officially discredited. Dismissed as romantic paranoia.

But Nara had always paid attention to fringe data. The anomalies. The pattern outliers that didn't behave.

And what disturbed her most was this:

The imprint didn't feel wrong. It felt... beautiful.

She stared at her reflection in the wall glass. The tight knot of hair. The fine lines around her eyes — not from age, but from clenched composure.

She touched her lips without thinking.

And a whisper of sensation returned. That kiss again.

That wanting again.

Only now, it came with a word. A name.

"Tomas."

Spoken not in her own voice. But in someone else's.

Part II: The Sleeper

Lia came awake into the dream slowly.

The room was pale, the air citrus-clean. Sunlight poured through arched glass, and the floors beneath her feet hummed faintly with radiant warmth. There was silence, but not the kind she was used to — not the kind that meant loneliness or low power grid or hunger.

This was soft silence. Rich silence.

She moved through the apartment like she belonged there.

Every surface gleamed. The kitchen was bare but beautiful. A single orchid on the windowsill had been watered — yesterday. She could feel it.

She could feel everything. This wasn't a dream.

It was a simulation built from Nara's memory logs.

And Lia had learned to access it, little by little, after each RestShare cycle. At first it was accidental — a scent here, a flash of emotion there. Then she started saving the fragments. Rebuilding. Inserting herself into the missing moments.

Now, when she closed her eyes in sleep, she woke here. In Nara's life.

She made tea — just like Nara did. She knew the exact brand from the neural residue, the steeping time from Nara's muscle memory. She wore Nara's robe, touched her skin in the mirror, copied her smile — that

slight, almost unnoticeable upturn at the corner that said, "I'm fine, I
don't need you."

But Lia did need someone.

And lately, that someone had become Tomas.

In the dream, he entered the room like he always did — barefoot,
distracted, beautiful.

He didn't speak at first. He never did in the beginning. Just looked at
her like she was an echo he'd been trying to place.

She liked that look.

And today — today he crossed the room, touched her cheek. "Nara," he
whispered.

Her throat caught.

She wanted to tell him. I'm not her. I'm just the girl who sleeps your
wife's dreams. But I remember everything now. Every breath. Every
moment she stopped loving you and didn't say it. Every look you gave
her that she didn't return.

She didn't say it. Instead, she leaned in. And he kissed her.

The dream shimmered.

A pulse of something cold ran through the air. Not from her, but from
far away. A disturbance. A watcher.

And in the kiss, Tomas pulled back — not abruptly, but slowly. He
looked into her eyes.

And for the first time, said something unscripted. "You're not her."

Lia woke up gasping in the clinic pod.

Heart pounding. Skin damp. Neural net humming with warning lights.

The technician pulled back from the monitoring console, frowning.

"That shouldn't happen," they muttered.

Lia said nothing.

She curled in on herself, tears burning the back of her eyes.

Because for a second — a single, precious second — she had been her.

And now, Nara knew.

Part III: The Mirror and the Door

NARA

She saw the anomaly in the neural report just after noon.

"Unscheduled REM spike – Lia R. | Duration: 00:03:14 | Unauthorized
Memory Sync Attempt Detected."

Unauthorized.

Three minutes of breach — while Nara's body was awake and moving.

She touched her own skin, absently. Rubbed her wrists. Checked the
mirrors in three different rooms. She wasn't sure what she expected to
find.

But it was there — a lingering presence. A borrowed intimacy. Not an
attack.

More like... a caress.

She initiated a formal request: donor image release.

It would ping Lia's clinic — grant Nara the right, for the first time, to see
her. She didn't know why she needed to.

But when the file arrived, her breath hitched.

The girl was young. Pale. Tired around the eyes. Fine-boned. Fragile-looking, but not in a weak way — in the way of someone used to surviving.

There was an intelligence there, too. A depth.

And something else Nara couldn't name. It wasn't envy.

It wasn't guilt.

It was something she hadn't felt in years. Vulnerability.

LIA

She sat alone in her recovery booth, trembling.

The technician had told her the sync error would be flagged. There'd be consequences. RestShare clients didn't like to be touched — not really.

They wanted function, not presence. Sleep, not spirit.

But Nara hadn't locked her out.

Not yet.

Not completely.

And that meant maybe... Maybe she felt it too.

That soft merging. That warmth Lia had tasted — not just from Tomas, but from the life itself. The smell of jasmine and ink in the home. The curve of the mug handle. The quiet between words. It was like living in poetry.

And Lia didn't want to give it up.

She opened her sketchpad.

A rough charcoal drawing: Nara's face. Not as it was.

But as it felt.

Lia traced the curve of the jaw. The eyes. The mouth she had kissed in a dream. She didn't draw Tomas.

She drew her.

Because it wasn't about him anymore. It was about becoming.

NARA

She opened the back-channel chat at 18:00 — something no sponsor was ever supposed to do.

But she'd stared at Lia's file all afternoon. Had reread her medical history.

Her creative output. Her dream patterns. She'd felt her.

And now she needed to know. She typed:

"Lia. What are you doing to me?" There was no typing indicator.

No reply.

And then:

"I think I love you."

Part IV: Entanglement

The First Contact (Nara & Lia — Private Channel) The message lingered in Nara's feed like a bruise. "I think I love you."

She stared at it for minutes, maybe longer, her finger hovering over the reply window. She hadn't expected that.

Not that.

Tomas hadn't used the word in weeks.

And here it was, dropped gently but fearlessly by a stranger who had only known her in sleep.

No — not a stranger.

A girl who had been inside her. Her thumbs hovered.

Then typed:

"You don't know me." A pause.

Then:

"I know how you feel when you're alone."

"I know how your skin remembers things your mind forgets."

"I know you keep a sweater you never wear because it belonged to someone who made you feel real."

Nara froze.

She had that sweater.

Hadn't worn it in three years. How—

She cut the chat. Instantly. Almost violently. But the tremble in her chest didn't stop.

The Confrontation (Virtual Reality Sync)

Nara initiated the override. She had rights.

Lia was a RestShare donor under active contract. And after the breach — the imprint, the messaging — Nara was within legal scope to request a direct virtual sync. Supervised, recorded, emotionally filtered.

But Nara disabled the filters. And did it alone.

The room rendered around her — a neutral white cube. Basic geometry, low resolution to minimize interference.

Lia appeared across from her a second later. Barefoot. Plain clothes. No makeup. Smaller in person than Nara expected. And not afraid.

Not even slightly.

Nara stepped forward. "Why did you message me?" Lia tilted her head. "You messaged me first."

"That wasn't permission."

"No," Lia said. "It was curiosity."

Nara folded her arms. "You're violating contract boundaries. Emotional syncing is forbidden."

Lia shrugged. "Then stop sleeping through me." Nara's breath caught. "I didn't ask you to be inside my dreams." "No," Lia said. "You just rented them." Silence.

Tension thickened between them — not hostile but charged.

Lia stepped forward now, just a pace. "You feel things in me that you can't feel alone. That's not theft. That's resonance."

Nara's voice went cold. "You're fantasizing. Building stories out of sweat and sleep. That isn't love."

Lia looked straight at her.

"No," she said. "But it could've been."

Nara stepped closer. Only a foot between them now.

"You think you love me," she said. "But what you love is my absence. My shape. My life like a suit you tried on."

Lia smiled softly. "That might be true." Then, quietly:

"But I'm not the only one trying it on anymore. You kept my kiss. You let it stay. Why?"

Nara said nothing. Because there was no why. Only the memory.
The echo of wanting that didn't belong to her — but felt more real than anything she'd touched in months.
And now?
Now they stood there in virtual proximity — boundaryless, breathless, known — and the worst part was:
Nara didn't want the sync to end.

Part V: Dream Theft

The Day After the Sync Nara couldn't shake it. Not the words.
Not the feeling.
Not the way Lia had looked at her — like a mirror that wanted to crack itself open and step through.
She tried to resume normal routines. Client calls. Strategic briefs. But everything felt off- centre. Like someone had rearranged the furniture in her mind.
Even Tomas noticed.
"You've been quiet," he said that night, across the dinner table. Nara looked at him, his tired eyes, his wine-stained fingertips. And wondered, for a split second:
Who have you been kissing?

LIA

The sync had changed her.

Not just emotionally — biologically.

Her neural map had begun adapting to Nara's patterns. Reflex mimicry.

A known but rare side effect of prolonged RestShare.

Except Lia had gone further than the system allowed.

After the sync, she intercepted biometric metadata. Voice files. Gait recordings. Micro- expression clusters.

It wasn't difficult.

Nara's life was full of structure. Her identity, as precise as a formula.

And Lia was an artist.

She didn't want to hurt her. She just wanted a chance.

One Week Later

Nara received an alert.

[Device Login – Unauthorized Facial Auth Attempt] Location: Urban Clinic Node 17B (RestShare Hub) Flagged User: Lia R.]

She stared at the screen.

The system had stopped the breach.

But not before Lia had made it inside one of her subaccounts. Briefly.

Just long enough to download her speech training module. Her handwriting signature.

And a virtual access key. Nara's stomach turned. This wasn't affection. This was invasion.

She initiated an emergency recall of the RestShare contract. But the clinic flagged a conflict.

"Lia R. has been pre-authorized for continued sleep matching via external sponsor." "What sponsor?" Nara asked.

But the system gave her no name.

That night, Tomas didn't come home. He messaged her at 03:12 AM. "Staying at the gallery. Don't wait up." He never used to say that.

Nara didn't sleep.

LIA

The kiss wasn't the same when it was real. But it was close enough.

Tomas was kind. Vulnerable. He didn't ask questions. Lia didn't lie.

She just didn't correct him.

And when he whispered "Nara" into her hair, she said nothing.

NARA

The next morning, Nara looked in the mirror. She touched her lips.

And for a second — just a flicker — she felt someone else's mouth move with hers.

Her hand fell away.

She stared at her reflection and whispered the one name she swore she'd never say again.

But it wasn't Tomas. It was Lia.

And this time, the ache didn't fade. It bloomed.

~ * ~

About the Author

Roxanne V. writes dark, emotional, and thought-provoking stories that explore the complexities of love, regret, and humanity in a rapidly changing technological world. Based in London, she draws inspiration from moments of stillness and small heartbreaks. *Echoes of Tomorrow* is her debut collection.

This book was written in solitude, but it lives through connection.

If it moved you, confused you, haunted you, or made you feel something — I'd be deeply grateful if you left a short review on Amazon or Goodreads.

Thank you for reading.

Acknowledgements and thanks to:

My beloved cousin Liuba for supporting me no matter what.

Dawn Wright, the kindest woman on Earth, for being there for me.

The stories in this book are just the beginning.

Roxanne V. is continuing to explore the fragile edge between humanity and technology — but next time, expect sharper thoughts, stranger twists, and even a little humour in the face of darkness. Not every ending will break you. Some might make you laugh.

Roxanne V. is also working on a series of funny but with meaningful messages children's books soon to be released – be ready to check them out!

www.ingramcontent.com/pod-product-compliance
Lightning Source LLC
Chambersburg PA
CBHW020141150626
46552CB00021B/1074